SPECIAL MESSAGE TO READERS

THE ULVERSCROFT FOUNDATION
(registered UK charity number 264873)

was established in 1972 to provide funds for research, diagnosis and treatment of eye diseases. Examples of major projects funded by the Ulverscroft Foundation are:-

- The Children's Eye Unit at Moorfields Eye Hospital, London
- The Ulverscroft Children's Eye Unit at Great Ormond Street Hospital for Sick Children
- Funding research into eye diseases and treatment at the Department of Ophthalmology, University of Leicester
- The Ulverscroft Vision Research Group, Institute of Child Health
- Twin operating theatres at the Western Ophthalmic Hospital, London
- The Chair of Ophthalmology at the Royal Australian College of Ophthalmologists

You can help further the work of the Foundation by making a donation or leaving a legacy. Every contribution is gratefully received. If you would like to help support the Foundation or require further information, please contact:

THE ULVERSCROFT FOUNDATION
The Green, Bradgate Road, Anstey
Leicester LE7 7FU, England
Tel: (0116) 236 4325

website: www.foundation.ulverscroft.com

DANCE OF DANGER

Injured ballet dancer Sonia returns to her family home, Alderburn Hall, to discover that her cousin Juliette is dead. Clues point to Lewis, Juliette's widower, being responsible — yet Sonia still finds herself falling in love with him ... Several mysterious 'accidents' threaten not only her, but also Lewis's small daughter. Is Sonia in true danger? Can she discover the culprit? And can she and Lewis ever count on a future together?

EVELYN ORANGE

DANCE OF DANGER

Complete and Unabridged

LINFORD
Leicester

First published in Great Britain in 2013

First Linford Edition
published 2014

Copyright © 2011 by Evelyn Orange
All rights reserved

A catalogue record for this book is available
from the British Library.

ISBN 978–1–4448–2227–4

Published by
F. A. Thorpe (Publishing)
Anstey, Leicestershire

Set by Words & Graphics Ltd.
Anstey, Leicestershire
Printed and bound in Great Britain by
T. J. International Ltd., Padstow, Cornwall

This book is printed on acid-free paper

1

Sonia Landale stepped down from the bus at the village green in Alderburn, taking care not to jar her leg. It was like entering a dream, to be back in the place she grew up after all these years. How her life had changed in that time!

Taking her mobile phone from her pocket, she dialled the number of Alderburn House once more.

'*This is Lewis Gordon. We are sorry we are unable to take your call, but if you'd like to leave a message, please speak after the tone.*'

Pressing the disconnect button, Sonia frowned. She had hoped that it would be different this time. For three weeks she had been trying to make contact, but all she ever heard was this message recorded by her cousin's husband. It was just as well she had left her suitcase at the Left Luggage at Durham rail station. There was no point in hiring a taxi, as it was less than two miles if she took the track by the stile, and then the country lanes. It shouldn't be too rough, especially as her physio had said that it would be good for her to walk. He probably hadn't meant on muddy paths, but she didn't have much choice.

A year ago she wouldn't have given the walk a second thought. Then she had been a soloist with the Southern Ballet, living in London and in love with her dance partner, Richard. But it had all changed one wet night, when she returned early from a tour in Germany. Richard had stayed behind because he was preparing the choreography for a new short ballet. Sonia had expected to be away for six weeks, but four weeks into the tour she had twisted her ankle and decided to come home. She hadn't phoned Richard, aiming to surprise him.

But instead it was Sonia who had been rudely surprised. She had found her cousin Juliette at Richard's flat, and it was clear from their state of undress that they had been in bed together. In dismay she had run from the flat, but slipped on the stairs, breaking her leg badly. Despite intensive rehabilitation, her ballet career was now over.

Sonia had spent the past eight months recuperating with her mother and step-father in Canada. It was her mother who had finally persuaded her to face Juliette. Sonia had sent a letter, emailed, and had tried ringing several times, but always reached the answerphone. But she was here now and, whether or not she was welcome, she had to go through with it. In any case, she wanted to see her grandmother, as Sonia knew that the rift had upset her.

Now that she was approaching the house, Sonia knew that it wouldn't be easy. A small knot of dread began to form within her, just as she felt a large spot of rain on her cheek. Almost immediately a downpour began, and she quickened her pace, feeling the strain in her weakened leg. It began to ache insistently.

The rain pattered loudly on the trees as she pulled her collar up round her ears. Maybe that was why she didn't hear the car approaching until it was upon her and could only dive into the hedge as it roared round the corner at a ridiculous speed. She was aware of a flash of red as the low saloon, built for speed, surged away without pausing.

'Stupid idiot,' she shouted, thinking worse in her mind, as she rubbed her leg, which had been jarred by her jump. Pulling twigs from her clothes, Sonia doubted that the driver had even noticed her. At that speed the hedge-rows must have been a blur, her green jacket blending into the background. A sharp pain stabbed through her right leg at each step. Pausing for breath, she saw thankfully that the field track was still open. She slipped through the walkers' gate.

The rain came on heavier, soaking her hair. The new red tint she'd had done in London was effectively ruined. What a state to be in to confront her cousin, when she'd wanted to be confident. With each step Sonia wished she had taken the taxi from Durham. What did a few pounds matter, after all? She was shivering by this time, nausea from the increasing pain in her leg making her head spin.

At last she struggled through the mud to the bridge across the river. It was in full spate. The house was now visible beyond the trees, a light winking to welcome her through the dusk. Limping painfully, it seemed an eternity before she reached the front door. She pulled on the bell urgently, thankful that there were lights on indoors. Someone at least must be at home.

It was a long time before her ring was answered, and she was already reaching out to the bell again when the door opened a crack, barely revealing a shadowed figure in the hallway. There was a muffled whisper. It sounded like 'Juliette.'

'Hello — it's Sonia. Nobody met the train — I wasn't sure . . . '

'My God, Sonia!' It was spat out with venom. Lewis Gordon, Juliette's husband, flung open the front door. His eyes, which had only ever looked at her with kindness, were hard and unwelcoming. 'What are you doing here now? Today, of all days. Couldn't wait to get your hands on your inheritance?'

Sonia stood dumbfounded, the rain trickling down her neck from her soaked hair. 'I don't understand. What's happened?'

His face contorted with anger. 'Don't try that with me. Of course you know — that's why you're here, isn't it?'

'Know what? Tell me, Lewis. I've no idea what you mean.'

The clean-cut planes of his face were gaunt and unforgiving, totally unlike the warm person she remembered. 'Juliette's dead. If you didn't know, then you should have.'

'Dead?' Sonia whispered incredulously. She couldn't take it in. Pain and exhaustion overcame her, blackness rushing in to claim her as she crumpled at his feet.

★ ★ ★

'It's incredible, she looks so like Juliette. No wonder Lewis mistook her. What a shock it must have given him.'

The voice drifted into her consciousness.

'She's waking up.'

Sonia took a deep breath, shivering. Finally the room ceased spinning, and she was able to focus on the woman's face bending over her. The features were refined, a strong face with a full mouth, made up perfectly.

'Michaela.' Sonia reached out to pull herself upright. 'Tell me it's not true! What Lewis said . . . She can't be dead.'

Her father's cousin, Michaela, who had lived at Alderburn for most of her life, now sat back, her hands twisting the ends of the black scarf at her neck. 'Oh, Sonia, my dear, it *is* true, I can't deny it. The . . . the funeral was today. It's been a harrowing day . . . a harrowing few weeks.'

Sonia fought to make sense of the

words, feeling the beginnings of a dull ache of loss. Then she became aware of a bowed figure sitting in the chair opposite. 'Granny!' she exclaimed. 'Why didn't you let me know? I would have come earlier.'

Felicity Landale barely acknowledged her granddaughter. The soft folds of skin dragged down her cheeks and the corners of her mouth into lines of despair. Then she shook her head slowly, gazing at Sonia with sad eyes. 'Tell her, Michaela.' Sonia had never heard her grandmother's voice sound so thin and weak.

'It was so tragic.' Michaela shook her head, as if she could hardly believe the facts. 'It was April — just after Easter. We'd had a lot of rain; the river was in spate. They found her body just outside Alderburn.'

Sonia was aghast. 'What do you mean . . . that she *drowned?*' Michaela nodded. 'But she was a strong swimmer — how could she possibly . . . ?'

'We all thought it was an accident at

first. Her head was bruised — she must have hit it when she fell into the river. Then Lewis found the note.'

There was a silence as Sonia took in the implications of these words. 'I don't believe it. You're trying to tell me she . . . it was suicide? Juliette? No, no, it's impossible.'

Michaela gripped Sonia's hands. 'It's true, dear. There was no doubt about it. The coroner said the evidence was irrefutable.'

'I just can't believe . . . Not Juliette. No-one could have more zest for life than she did.'

'There was no doubt at all.' Michaela was vehement in her emphasis. She went over to the window, the heels of her black court shoes tapping on the polished hardwood floor. She loosened the ties on the chintz curtains at the side window, drawing them across to shut out the dusk, then turned round. 'Her note . . . ' A frown appeared between her neatly shaped brows. 'It was an apology to Lewis, and not to let

Kirsty think too badly of her, something like that.'

Sonia had momentarily forgotten Juliette and Lewis's young daughter. 'Poor Kirsty. How is she taking it?'

'All she knows is that Mummy went to heaven and she won't be seeing her for a very long time.'

'She's five now, isn't she?'

'Yes, that's right. Poor little thing's very confused, naturally. We've tried to keep her away from the press, but they've been so persistent, it was horrendous.'

'Ghouls!' came the biting comment from Felicity. Sonia jumped. She'd almost forgotten the old lady was still there, sitting like a statue in the firelight. As if in reply to her bitter outburst, a log cracked loudly in the grate.

'So that's why the telephone wasn't answered.'

Michaela nodded. 'Yes, we stopped listening to the messages.'

' . . . And my letter? It must have arrived around the time of . . . of . . . '

'We never saw any letter. But of

course, we haven't cleared her things yet. Did you address it to Juliette?'

'Yes. I posted it from Canada, before I flew over. My mother's address was on it, but they moved house the week after I left. I sent an email as well.'

Michaela sat down in the other armchair, crossing her elegant legs. 'It's many years since I saw your mother — probably at Juliette's wedding. How is she?'

Sonia shivered. How could Michaela speak her cousin's name so casually already? She supposed they had grown used to her death over the past few weeks.

'Mum? Oh, she's fine. She teaches art at a school in Edmonton, and is still enjoying it. Dan's still a college administrator.'

'You like your stepfather, don't you?' Michaela seemed to relax, easing back into the chair.

'Yes, we get on fine.' Suddenly feeling the need to be alone, she swung her feet off the settee on to the floor. 'Would you mind if I stay here tonight?'

Michaela stood up quickly. 'As soon as I saw you, I asked Mrs. Howe to prepare your old room. We don't use the main guest room any more.'

Sonia nodded gratefully and stood up to follow Michaela. On her way out she bent to kiss her grandmother's papery cheek. The familiar faded French perfume floated into her nostrils. She smiled. Felicity responded with a gentle curve of the lips, taking her grand-daughter's hand in a tight grip. 'I'm glad you're here,' she murmured, too softly for Michaela to hear. 'Now we can get to the bottom of all this.'

Sonia opened her lips to make a startled comment, but was silenced as the old lady put one finger over her own closed mouth. Seeing that Sonia under-stood her gesture, she nodded, smiled, then closed her eyes, relinquishing her grip.

'Goodnight, Granny,' she said softly, and followed Michaela. The hallway was looking shabbier than it had done when Sonia had last visited Alderburn five years earlier, at the time of Kirsty's christening. The hardwood floor had virtually lost its polished surface, despite the valiant attentions of Mrs. Howe, who had the glorious title of house-keeper, but was little more than a daily help and cook these days.

'I hope you'll find the nursery suite comfortable enough,' Michaela remarked as they ascended the stairs to the first floor. 'It has been in use — Kirsty's nanny lived there until last week.'

'Where is she now?' Sonia pulled her-self up the stairs awkwardly, trying not to jar her aching leg. She saw Michaela's eyes flicker to her leg and away again, as if embarrassed by her disability.

'Oh, the silly girl quit when the media attention started. As if we didn't have enough to contend with without her leaving us in the lurch.'

Michaela had never had much time for young children. Although she had been at Alderburn all the years that Juliette and Sonia had been growing up, she had only become friendly with them when they had passed into their teens, and could be treated as young adults.

Michaela had come to live at Alderburn Hall with Felicity and her husband Michael at the age of ten. Her father had been serving abroad in the army, and when he died tragically in a training accident, her mother had quickly remarried, clearly glad to leave her daughter at Alderburn. Felicity and Michael had been parents to her, and she had never married despite a number of admirers. She had been engaged once, but Sonia suspected that she had been the one to break it off. She had always thought that Michaela enjoyed living at the big house and spending her money on herself.

'Kirsty's in bed,' Michaela whispered as they crossed the landing to the nursery wing. They entered a corridor, which led to the two bedrooms that had been Juliette's and Sonia's when they were growing up. The larger room, once

Juliette's, was now occupied by her small daughter. Sonia had always slept in the other room when she returned to Alderburn, until Kirsty had been born and the nanny had used it.

Michaela pulled the window shut with a snap, as the air was cool. 'Will you be all right here? There are fresh towels in the bathroom.'

Sonia sank onto the coverlet of the bed, thankful to ease her aching leg. 'I'll be fine, thanks.' It would be a relief to be alone, to digest the events of the past hour. As Michaela crossed back to the door, Sonia swivelled round. 'I'm sorry about my unexpected arrival, today of all days. You needn't worry. I won't upset things by staying. I'll make other arrangements tomorrow.'

Michaela paused, her expression strange and unfathomable. 'But my dear, you of all people have the right to stay.'

'What . . . what do you mean?'

'What Lewis said, about claiming your inheritance. You didn't realise?'

Sonia rubbed her forehead with the

back of one hand, suddenly confused. 'He was angry and upset. He thought for a moment I was Juliette.'

Thoroughly composed, a little smile on her lips, Michaela shook her head. 'What he said was true. We read the will this afternoon. Alderburn Hall is yours — Juliette left it to you.'

2

Sonia awoke to full daylight, surprised to find that she had slept for so long. Opening one eye, she registered that her bedside clock said five past eight. There was no need to get up yet.

It had taken some time to get to sleep last night, the shocks of the day revolving in her mind. She found her cousin's suicide the most difficult to understand. Juliette was the last person she could have imagined taking her own life.

Then Sonia became aware of a small figure standing in the doorway. She sat up abruptly.

'Kirsty?' The little girl, wearing a pale blue dressing gown, clutched a grey stuffed rabbit tightly under one arm. Her dark hair, shining with glints of her mother's auburn, hung loose on her shoulders.

'Are you my Auntie Sonia?'

'Yes, I am. Hello.' She smiled at the child, pushing her own tousled hair back behind her ears.

Satisfied at her identity, Kirsty stepped into the room. 'Have you brought my mummy with you? When's she coming home?'

Sonia's heart gave a lurch of dread. How did she cope with this? 'Well . . . Kirsty, Mummy's not with me. She's in heaven. What did they tell you?'

The child seemed unfazed by this explanation, and came over to the bed. 'Yes, I know she went to heaven. But I thought you might have brought her with you.'

Sonia's only thought was to get away from the subject as quickly as possible. She had no idea what to do with a five-year-old child, especially if she started to cry. 'No, not this time, dear. But maybe you and I could do something nice this morning. How would you like that?' She smiled encouragingly.

'Would you like to see my kitten?

Daddy bought her for me last week.'

'A kitten! Aren't you lucky! Yes, I'd love to see her. Let's both get dressed, then we can go and find her.'

Kirsty nodded and was happy to let her help with dressing, choosing bright yellow leggings and a matching T-shirt with a cartoon lion on the front. While Kirsty put on her trainers, Sonia threw on her jeans and T-shirt, then took the little girl down the nursery stairs to the breakfast room.

The table was set with three places. The evidence of a few crumbs showed that one had already been cleared — obviously Lewis had left for his office earlier. He was a senior partner in a solicitors in Durham. It was a relief not to have to face him again so soon after their disastrous meeting last night.

When Sonia was small there had been maids, a cook, and gardeners at the hall. Generations ago the Landales had once been mine-owners in the region, but the coming of nationalisation had taken that from them. Her grandfather's father had been quite successful in using the compensation money, but Michael Landale had not had his father's financial acumen. Bad investment losses just before his death, followed by the young demise of Sonia's father and his twin brother, had left the estate severely depleted. Sonia's and Juliette's fathers had been killed in a mountaineering accident when Sonia was only eleven, her cousin two years older.

For many years the occupants of the house had run it mainly on a do-it-yourself basis, with the help of their stalwart part-time housekeeper, Mrs. Howe. No doubt it was she who had laid out breakfast this morning on the sideboard.

Sonia now poured out some cereal and milk for Kirsty, and was cutting some bread to toast for herself, when she heard a heavy tread in the corridor. Turning quickly, she saw a middle-aged woman approaching with a covered tray.

'Sonia, dear, how are you?' Her

round face was creased into a delighted smile.

'Hello, Mrs. Howe. I'm a bit tired, but not too bad. This has all been such . . . ' She paused, looking towards Kirsty, who was happily demolishing her cereal, but watching both the adults.

Mrs. Howe nodded gravely. 'I know. It's new for you. But life has to go on, especially for the sake of the kiddie.' Her voice changed almost to a chirp. 'And how's my poppet this morning? Isn't it nice that your auntie's come to visit?'

Kirsty smiled up at her. 'We're going to see Mitten after breakfast. Auntie Sonia likes kittens.'

'That's lovely, dear. But you'll need to be quick, because Daddy wants to take Auntie Sonia into Durham today. There's business to be seen to. But she'll be coming back later. You're to come shopping with me and then Nicola's coming to play with you.'

Seeing Sonia's bemused expression,

she explained. 'Nicola's a girl from the village. She's sixteen, and wants to be a nursery nurse. She's helping us out for a while until we sort out a new nanny.'

Sonia finished buttering her toast and sat down at the table next to Kirsty. Mrs. Howe laid the tray, obviously brought down from Felicity's room, on the sideboard while she added the dirty dishes from the table.

'Where's Michaela? Is this one of her days at the gallery?' Sonia asked.

Michaela worked for three days a week at a small art gallery in Durham. It had always been more of a hobby than a job, but she was good at her work.

'Miss Landale works most days now. I'm not sure if she's there today — it varies. But she went out quite early, no breakfast, as usual, just a cup of coffee.' Mrs. Howe pursed her lips disapprovingly. Then her face softened as she turned to Kirsty. 'Finished, my pet? You can show Auntie Sonia your kitten now.'

Sonia hastily swallowed her toast and the last of her orange juice, then allowed Kirsty to drag her along to the utility room. The kitten, a little ball of tabby and white fur with needle-sharp claws, was duly admired and cuddled. They amused the little animal for a while with a fishing-rod style toy, the child clapping and laughing with glee as it tumbled and pounced. Then Mrs. Howe announced that she was ready to go into Alderburn, so Kirsty raced upstairs to find her shoes.

At that moment the doorbell rang. As there was no-one else around to answer it, Sonia went to open it. She found herself facing a tall young woman of about her own age, her blonde hair short enough to be untouched by the wind. At Sonia's appearance she gasped, her hand flying to her throat. Then she relaxed.

'Oh, dear, you gave me such a fright there — for a moment I thought it was Juliette.'

'I'm her cousin, Sonia.'

'That explains the resemblance. I'm Laura Kendall. Juliette and I were in the operatic society together. I thought I might catch Lewis. He said last night he would be likely to be at home some time this morning.'

'We're expecting him back very soon. Would you like to wait?'

Laura gave a sigh, disappointment settling on her features. 'No, it's not really necessary. I expect you could help. I wondered if I could borrow Juliette's opera score for *Eugene Onegin*. She sang one of the arias at our last concert.'

'You'd better come in. I expect it's in the music room.'

Laura seemed to know her way about the house, crossing the hall to the sunny music room confidently. Juliette's opera scores were kept in the mahogany bookcase near the baby grand piano. The lid of the piano was now shut, its surface gleaming with polish. Obviously Mrs. Howe had been at work. Sonia joined Laura in scanning the scores.

'It's by Tchaikovsky,' Laura told her.

'I know,' Sonia stated tersely. She'd danced in a ballet version of the opera many times. After a few moments she added, 'I'm sorry, it doesn't seem to be there.'

Laura bit her lip. 'Oh, dear. I'd hoped to try the aria to see if it suits my voice before buying my own copy straight away. The music is rather difficult.'

'I'll have a look around later today, and if I find it, I'll ring you. Could you give me your number?'

'Lewis will tell you it. Or you could pop round with the score. My mother is often in during the day.'

'Where do you live?'

Laura looked at her incredulously. 'You mean you don't know? We're living at Alderfield Farm.'

The farmhouse was barely a quarter of a mile from Alderburn Hall. 'I thought it was a ruin,' Sonia said.

With a laugh, Laura pushed back her fringe, exposing a hint of darker roots. 'Hardly — We bought the farmhouse and some of the land for my horses, and the renovation was finished just after Christmas.'

'I see.' Sonia felt as if they were sparring at every word.

On the doorstep, Laura turned back. 'Would you tell Lewis . . . I'll telephone him at the weekend about the next meeting of the Conservation Society. He'll know what I'm talking about.' She smiled enigmatically, dangling her car keys in a farewell wave as she crossed to her red car.

Sonia felt a rush of resentment. This young woman seemed to be laying claim to Lewis, yet it was only a few weeks since his wife had died. Was there something going on between them, and had that precipitated Juliette's death? Maybe Lewis's anger at Sonia's arrival had been because he feared that she might discover something. And was it Laura's red car that had so nearly run her down in the lane yesterday? As she closed the door, her mind was whirling.

As Sonia reached the nursery wing, Kirsty skipped past her, singing a little tune under her breath on her way to join Mrs. Howe. Sonia couldn't help smiling at the sound as she applied a touch of lipstick. Glancing at her watch, she noticed that it was barely half past nine. Lewis was to collect her at ten o'clock, so she decided to go back downstairs to wait in the music room.

As she passed Juliette and Lewis's bedroom, she thought about the score that Laura wanted, and decided to take a quick look. The room seemed quite bare. The bed was made up with a floral throw, neat and smooth. The dressing table, once overflowing with Juliette's trinkets and bottles, now held a single china dish.

Crossing quickly to the chest of drawers, she pulled them open one by one. It felt eerie doing this, knowing that Juliette would never return. They contained nothing but clothes — beautiful silk and lace underwear in the top drawers, woollen sweaters and cotton tops in the lower drawers. They weren't very full. Someone, maybe Michaela, must have started to empty them. An immense sense of loss suddenly overwhelmed her. Despite Juliette's occasional selfishness, they had grown up like sisters. It seemed impossible that she was gone.

After a few minutes she stirred herself out of her reverie. There was only one place left to look. In the wardrobe she found some of Juliette's clothes still hanging, exuding a faint perfume as the door slid open. At the bottom were several shoeboxes. Sonia knelt down carefully, to avoid jarring her injured leg, and rummaged amongst them. Most of the boxes were empty. Of the Tchaikovsky music there was no sign. She stood up slowly, helping herself by pulling on the door handle.

'What do you think you're doing?'

At the sound of Lewis's angry voice, she swung round guiltily. He stood in the doorway, his suit jacket over one shoulder. His grey eyes were narrowed in fury. He strode into the bedroom, drawing his full six feet of height over Sonia.

28

'Lewis . . . I'm sorry, it must look awful . . . '

'You bet it does. What are you doing in Juliette's wardrobe, for God's sake?'

'It was Laura Kendall . . . she wanted me to look for a music score, an opera she wanted to borrow. It wasn't in the music room, and I thought it might be in here . . . I'm sorry, I should have asked first.' Her voice trailed off lamely.

'There was no need,' he stated curtly. 'After all, it *is* your house.' At that he turned on his heel, and made to leave.

'Lewis . . . '

He paused, looking at her questioningly.

'Lewis, please, I didn't know about the house. I didn't even know about Juliette. I . . . I came back to talk with her. I'm sorry.'

For a moment he hesitated, then the lines of anger on his face smoothed away. He shook his head. 'Just stop apologising.' He wasn't exactly friendly, but at least he seemed to have calmed down. 'I'll see you downstairs as soon as you're ready. There are papers to be signed in Durham.'

She smarted at his peremptory manner. 'If we have time, I'd like to collect my case from the station.'

He nodded, turning abruptly on his heel. Their uneasy silence continued through the journey to Durham as the silver BMW glided down the small lanes. Sonia watched Lewis's movements out of the corner of her eyes. It was difficult to recall the easy camaraderie they had once shared, the spark of attraction that had always been there between them, despite his marriage to her cousin. The planes of his face seemed sharper, making him look older; a man who had been through hard times. Reminding herself that he had just lost his wife in the most awful circumstances, her anger began to dissipate.

Sonia retrieved her case from the luggage locker where she had deposited it the day before. Then Lewis drove her down the road to the centre of the city and parked by his practice. The ubiquitous tourists and students milled around them, photographing the castle and the Norman cathedral, or gazing down at the riverbanks.

As they entered the vestibule they met a broad, white-haired man in the uniform solicitor's grey suit, pouring coffee for himself.

'This is my partner, Bill Kendall. Bill, my wife's cousin, Sonia Landale.'

The older man extended a large hand to shake hers.

Sonia started at the name. 'Are you any relation to Laura Kendall?'

He smiled. 'So you know my gorgeous girl, do you?'

'She called at the hall this morning. She was looking for some music that she wanted to borrow.'

'Ah, yes. Laura's so dedicated to her singing. Lovely voice. Have you heard her sing?'

'No, not yet . . . '

Lewis interrupted the conversation. 'I've brought Sonia along to sign the papers to do with the hall, Bill.'

Immediately Bill Kendall's features took on a reverent solemnity. 'Of course. Dreadful business. I'll get them at once, Lewis. Will you come this way, please.'

Lewis followed as Bill Kendall ushered them into his office. The offices were converted from an eighteenth-century building, but despite their age, the rooms were light and airy, decorated in pale colours. An antique print of Durham Cathedral hung behind Bill's desk. His secretary brought the relevant files, smiling warmly, then returned to her own office.

'Now, Miss Landale . . . or may I call you Sonia?' Bill was obviously turning on the charm. She smiled and nodded.

Bill continued. 'What do you know about the legacy?'

'Well, all I know is that Michaela told me last night that Juliette had left me the hall.'

Kendall looked apologetic. 'Ah, that's not strictly true.'

Sonia turned in surprise to Lewis. 'But everyone said . . .'

'Juliette left the house jointly to you and Kirsty,' Lewis explained.

'But why to me at all? Surely it should have gone completely to Kirsty?'

'I suspect she always thought that you had some right to the house,' Lewis told her. 'After all, your fathers were twins. Even though your father was the younger brother, and wasn't brought up to inherit the hall, he always loved it more than Juliette's father did. Then there was the general family feeling that it was Paul's fault that they died on that mountaineering trip to Mont Blanc. I believe it took a lot of persuading to get Aidan to go with him.'

Sonia couldn't deny this, and gave in. Lewis showed her where to sign, and added his own signature on Kirsty's behalf. Afterwards, as they drove back to Alderburn Hall, Sonia felt that he was gentler. He finally broke their silence at their approach to the hall.

'I'm sorry I've been so unwelcoming.

It hasn't been easy these past few weeks. The reporters really drove me spare. I suppose I needed someone to lash out at, and you happened to be in the line of fire. I hope you'll forgive me.'

Relieved, Sonia gave a small smile. 'Of course I will. I did arrive unexpectedly. If I'd known about . . . all this . . . I would have done things very differently.'

He nodded, his expression kinder, more like the Lewis she recalled and had always liked. 'Don't overdo things with that leg today.' They drew up at the front door.

Sonia stepped out. 'Oh, Lewis, I just remembered. Laura gave me a message for you. She said she'd telephone about the meeting of the Conservation Society this weekend.'

His expression clouded. 'What next? Laura's always trying to rope me in for something, and this is her latest idea. She was round here two or three times a week when they first moved in.'

'Was she Juliette's friend?'

He gave a bark of laughter. 'In a way — but more a rival than a friend. They always competed for the lead roles in the operatic society, and Juliette always got them. Still, I think they found a lot in common. Michaela's taken to her, had her round for a meal once or twice. No doubt she'll turn up again soon.'

Sonia nodded. Before she closed the car door, she thought of something. 'Lewis — would you mind if I play the piano in the music room?'

'Of course not. The more normal things are, for Kirsty's sake, the better.'

Once he had returned to Durham and she had the house to herself, she decided to indulge her whims and play the baby grand piano. She had played for pleasure for many years, and it had been something that had kept her going through her convalescence. All Juliette's music was on the shelves nearest to the piano. Sonia chose some Chopin, a nocturne that she knew, and began to play.

Scarcely had she launched into a cascade of notes, when there was a startled gasp behind her.

'My God . . . Juliette!'

A strange man stood by the door, white-faced with shock.

3

The newcomer stood at about Lewis's height, and had dark hair, but there the similarities ended. Lewis kept himself fit with regular visits to the gym, and tennis at weekends, but this young man was positively muscular. His hair curled almost to his shoulders, and his skin had the golden hue of one who spent long hours out of doors. His light blue T-shirt was taut across his chest. But his face now had a grey tinge beneath its tan, and his brown eyes were troubled.

'Don't be a fool, Tim. Of course it's not Juliette. It's our own Sonia, come home to claim her inheritance.'

Michaela's voice had a note of teasing as she took the young man's arm and escorted him into the music room. She wore a casual floral suit in black and white, and as usual her make-up was immaculate.

Sonia, her initial bewilderment disappearing, winced at Michaela's remark. 'You know that's not true, Michaela. Anyway, I'm only joint inheritor, with Kirsty.'

Michaela laughed. 'Don't be so touchy, dear. Now, let me introduce you to my young friend, Tim Warren. He's an artist from Australia who's staying in Durham at the moment.'

Tim seemed to have recovered his composure. He grinned, showing even, white teeth. 'Sorry, but you must admit there's a close resemblance. You almost gave me heart failure.'

Sonia smiled, feeling a little foolish at all the trouble her hair tint was causing. 'I'm not a natural redhead. It'll wash out in a few weeks.' She hurriedly changed the subject. 'So how long are you staying here?'

He shrugged his broad shoulders. 'Oh, as long as I feel I like it. I really like the area — not just the ancient history, but the sporting traditions, too.'

Sonia left the piano, limping towards

the window seat. 'What do you do? Oils, watercolour?'

'Acrylic is my medium, though I did quite a lot of sculpture back in Oz.' He displayed his spectacular teeth again.

'Tim's putting on an exhibition next month at the gallery. We're having lunch at the Alderburn Arms now. Care to join us?'

'Thanks, that would be nice. What about Kirsty?'

'The girl from the village, Nicola, or whatever her name is, will see to the child. Mrs. Howe returns at four o'clock.'

'And my grandmother?'

'I've taken up some lunch for her. She always comes down for supper, but will be quite happy dozing on her own without us fussing around her during the afternoon. She's not very mobile, these days.'

The gravel crunched under their feet as Tim led the way towards a sleek red car. It was a fast model, with only two doors. Sonia managed to manoeuvre her awkward leg into the back seat, while Michaela slipped into the passenger seat.

'You must be pretty successful to drive a car like this,' Sonia said to Tim.

'Oh, this little beaut belongs to Michaela. She lets me run it around for her from time to time.'

Sonia felt a shock as she caught the look that passed between the pair. Michaela's eyes were full of pride and warmth, like a lover. Michaela did look young for her age, but Tim must be almost twenty years younger. Still, she told herself, many older men were involved with young women. There was no need for her to feel shocked by the sexes being reversed.

Sonia soon found that Tim was good company, amusing her with stories of his life back in Australia. He made it sound such an exotic, exciting country. She found herself responding with information about her year in Canada.

'So you're making Alderburn your home now?' Tim asked while Michaela was buying another round of drinks. His eyes raked Sonia from head to foot, an openly appreciative look.

It was all she could do not to shift uncomfortably beneath his gaze and the directness of his question. 'I don't know.' She drew her finger round the circumference of a beer mat on the table. 'There's so much to take into consideration. It depends on whether Lewis wants me to stay.'

'Oh, come on! The house is half yours.'

'But it's been their home for over five years. I've been away for a long time. Still, there's a lot to discuss, so I'll have to stay for a while.'

'Well, at least we won't be losing the hall now.' Michaela lifted her glass of wine and looked into its ruby depths.

'Losing it?' Sonia's heart began to thump wildly.

'Juliette had been making enquiries about selling. I expect some of the agents will be getting in touch once they think an appropriate time has passed since the funeral.'

'But why? I hadn't heard anything about that before now.'

Tim set down his glass, licking the froth from his top lip. 'Lewis is so tight-mouthed, you'd have to squeeze any information out of him like the end of a tube of toothpaste.'

Michaela gave a splutter of laughter. 'Behave, Tim. I expect Lewis is also relieved that we're getting a reprieve. He adores the hall, and wants Kirsty to have it.'

'You won't consider selling, will you, Sonia?'

'I don't know what the real situation is, but of course I don't want to sell.'

Tim leaned over, grabbing her shoulder in a firm grip. 'Good girl. We're behind you.' His action took her by surprise. She couldn't think why Tim should care so much about Michaela's home — unless, of course, he was in love with her . . . She looked across at her quickly. Michaela was watching the two younger people over the rim of her glass, one side of her lips quirked upwards. Sonia couldn't read her expression at all.

After lunch, they dropped Sonia off at the hall, while Tim took Michaela back to his rented flat in Durham to look over some more pictures for his exhibition. Although she was invited to go with them, Sonia preferred to be on her own for a while. Michaela had always been a restless person, and Tim's energy seemed to spark her off.

She telephoned her mother later that evening to update her with the news. It calmed her to speak with her and her stepfather. Leaving the downstairs study, Sonia headed for the music room, but hesitated at the door when she saw Lewis in the window seat. His briefcase was beside him on the seat, where he had abandoned it to put his head in his hands, in a pose of abject despair.

Her breath caught in her throat. Not wishing to intrude, she stepped back, her hand still on the door. But Lewis had already heard her, and his head snapped up. His eyes were shadowed with tiredness.

'I'm sorry, I didn't know anyone was in here,' she stammered.

He stood up. 'Come in. I'm just going.' He bent down to retrieve his briefcase, and in doing so, dropped a large bulky brown envelope, which slid across the polished floor to land at Sonia's feet. She picked it up, holding it out to him. He stood looking at it, as if unsure what to do.

'What's wrong, Lewis?'

He ran his free hand through his hair. 'I picked that up from the police station this afternoon. They're the contents of Juliette's pockets and handbag . . . and the note she left me.'

'Oh, Lewis.' Sonia's heart contracted in sympathy.

He turned away from her abruptly. 'I expect you'll want to read it. Do what you like with it — but don't give it back to me. Get rid of it.' With that, he brushed past her and left the room before she could utter another word.

Sonia looked down at the envelope, feeling giddy with shock. How vulnerable Lewis had looked just now, his grief still fresh. It was at that moment she realised that she still felt a strong attraction to him. But she pulled herself up sharply — now was not the time to give it rein.

She decided to take the envelope up to her room. As she was passing her grandmother's room, a faint drift of perfume wafted into the corridor through the open door.

'Sonia dear, is that you?'

Smiling ruefully, Sonia pushed open the door. 'Yes, Granny. It's me.' There was no disguising her limp.

The old lady was seated in front of the fireplace in one of a pair of armchairs. No longer in the black she had worn yesterday, she looked much more like the grandmother Sonia had expected to see. She now wore tweed trousers with a cream silk blouse underneath a dark green woollen jacket. The face that was so dear to Sonia was more sunken now, and her grandmother's delicate hands clutched the arms of the chair like claws, tendons and veins clearly etched in the translucent skin. But she still had lovely blue eyes, which softened with love as she beckoned her granddaughter.

'Come and sit with me for a while. I haven't seen you all day. Are you recovered from your journey?'

Sonia took the chair opposite. A small electric heater had replaced the open fire that had once burned in the grate. Along the mantelpiece and on the surrounding wall were many framed photographs of her family. In pride of place was a picture of Juliette in an Edwardian ball gown in one of her shows. On the wall next to this was a portrait photo of Sonia as the Lilac Fairy in *Sleeping Beauty*. Sonia glanced away from this quickly as the familiar anguish stabbed her.

'I had a good night, thank you,' she said in reply to Felicity's question. 'But I feel — I feel I can never recover from the shock of discovering that Juliette killed herself. I just can't accept that she's gone. I expect her to walk round the next corner.'

Felicity nodded resignedly. 'It's been hard for all of us, though perhaps the little one is recovering most quickly. But of course, Juliette was always a distant mother. We knew her much more closely. She was a bright flame, a talented girl.'

'I shall miss her.'

'Even after the terrible thing she did to you?'

Sonia clenched her jaw. 'Yes, it was terrible, and it was worse because we had been so close. When I returned here I was prepared to forgive her, but only if she admitted that she realised how much she had hurt me, and took responsibility for her actions.'

Felicity shook her head with a fond smile. 'You should have stood up to her years earlier.'

'But she was always so glamorous to me, Granny. After all, I was three years younger, and it must have been a drag to her to be looking after her little cousin. I always did forgive her.'

'Well, maybe not everybody did . . . ' Felicity murmured.

'What was that?'

Her grandmother ignored the question. 'What's in your envelope, dear?'

Sonia smoothed the surface of the buff envelope with her hand. 'It's from the police. Lewis couldn't face opening it.'

'Juliette's things?'

Sonia nodded.

'Have you read the letter?' Felicity asked.

'No — I thought I would leave it until later. Though I feel almost like an intruder.'

'Open it. I want to know what you think.'

Sonia drew out a small white envelope. Lewis's name was scrawled on the front in Juliette's flamboyant handwriting. She took the note out and began to read.

Dear Lewis,

By the time you read this, I shall be long gone. Please don't be too angry with me for what I am doing. You know it's for the best. Things between us have deteriorated so much; I just can't live like this any more. I'm sorry to leave you all the muck about the hall, but you know better than I do how to sort it out.

Don't let Kirsty forget me. I know I haven't been a good mother, and she's better without me, but I do care about her. Maybe if you meet someone else she'll make a better mother than I did.

We did have some good times, didn't we?

Adieu.

Juliette.

Sonia sat quietly for a few moments after she had finished reading. 'Poor Lewis. No wonder he didn't want it back. He must feel so guilty.'

'Why do you say that?'

'Surely her words imply that it was the breakdown of their marriage that led her to take her own life. But it seems so unlike Juliette.'

There was a short silence. Then Felicity said, 'Sonia, dear . . . can you drive a car?'

Bewildered, as this seemed to have nothing to do with their conversation, she replied, 'Yes — as long as it's not too far, as my leg gets tired. Why?'

'I'd like you to take me into Durham on Sunday. I like going to evensong at the cathedral from time to time, and there's something I want to talk over with you.'

Sonia frowned. 'Can't we discuss it here? Anyway, I don't have a car.'

'I'll ask Lewis if you can drive Juliette's car. It's still in the garage.'

Her grandmother seemed to have ignored the first part of her question. But before she could repeat it, the old lady interrupted.

'There now, it's ten to seven. Time I readied myself for supper. Mrs. Howe always serves right on the hour. You'd better wash your hands, dear. Off you go now.'

Exasperated, but smiling at her swift relegation to childhood once more, Sonia kissed the worn cheek and picked up the envelope.

'What shall I do with the letter?'

'Give it to me. I'll keep it.' As Sonia looked at her quizzically, she added, 'You'll understand when we've had our little talk, dear.'

Felicity was as good as her word. The next morning, which was Saturday, Lewis called her into the study and gave her the keys to Juliette's car, a small Cabriolet model, only one year old.

'Just sign here on this form, and that will mean we can transfer the documents into your name. I've arranged some insurance for you.'

'But Lewis, I thought I was only to borrow the car,' she protested.

'You might as well have the use of it. It's no good to anyone else here.'

'Wouldn't you rather sell it?'

He smiled ruefully. 'I don't think you

realise what problems Juliette left you with the hall. You might as well get something from your legacy.'

Sonia sat down in the chair opposite his desk. 'People keep talking about Juliette wanting to sell. What's it all about?'

Lewis leaned back in his chair. 'I was hoping you'd be spared that for a while. Alderburn Hall is a beautiful early nineteenth century property, but it's been neglected for years, since your grandfather lost his money. Juliette's father also frittered away money on unsuccessful business ventures. Your parents at least had that small design business.'

'But Mum lost heart, and gave it up once I went to ballet school. That's when she trained as a teacher.'

Lewis nodded. 'There was enough money left in the estate to keep it afloat at first, but over the years the value of investments has fallen. The house has deteriorated so much now that it's reached the stage where significant money has to be spent on it, or else it'll become uninhabitable. Of course, we looked into all sorts of options, but Juliette had the ultimate say, and she decided to sell. Things quietened down when she died, but they can't be ignored for much longer.'

He didn't go into any further details, but Sonia was aware that they would also have more inheritance tax to pay. She was stunned. 'So it's true — we're going to lose the hall.'

Lewis leaned forward again, placing his elbows on the leather surface of the desk. As he looked straight at her, Sonia felt herself go limp with the surprising strength of her feelings for him. Her heart began to race, and her limbs trembled. Clenching her fists beneath the desk, she sat back, trying to submerge the intensity of her reaction. The attraction had always been there, but had never affected her as much as it did now. But she couldn't let it show. Even though they were both now free, Lewis was only recently widowed, and grieving.

'It's really up to you,' he began, ' . . . and me, as Kirsty's father. But I'm not willing to go ahead with the sale without further research. Juliette wouldn't give me the time I needed. She said she wanted to sell the place while we could still get a good price for it.'

'No wonder Michaela was horrified. Where would she go, and Granny?'

'Well, of course we always intended that your grandmother should have a home with us, but Michaela is perfectly capable of fending for herself. She's had things easy all her life. She's only ever used her earnings as pocket money, and she's never paid anything towards the upkeep of the house.'

'How long do you think we have before we have to make a decision one way or the other?'

'We may have six months to a year, while I investigate any grants or other financial sources. Shall I go ahead?'

Sonia faced him steadily. 'I don't want to lose the hall, Lewis. It's always been my family home.'

And, a small voice added inside her, it would keep her nearer to Lewis for a while.

4

'I hear Felicity's roped you in to take her to evensong at Durham. She hasn't been to the cathedral since we all went to the Christmas Eve service. I wondered if she would ever go there again.'

Sonia whirled round to face Michaela. 'Granny's deteriorated a lot since I last saw her. I never really thought of her as being old, until now.'

Michaela nodded. 'Felicity's had some severe blows in her life. Losing both her sons soon after her husband, and now her granddaughter . . . I think she's getting too old to bounce back.'

Sonia sighed. 'I know.'

Michaela suddenly smiled brightly. 'Still, it's done her good, you turning up. So, what are you doing until then? Would you like to come for a drive with Tim and me? We were thinking of driving up to Hexham, maybe even to the Roman Wall. Do come. Oh, there's Tim now.' Michaela's features lit up as a motorbike roared up to the front door.

Sonia was sorely tempted. She'd loved Hadrian's Wall country as a child, and longed to see it again. But there was some sort of undercurrent between Michaela and Tim that she couldn't place. She didn't want to intrude on their relationship.

'It's very kind of you, Michaela, but I think I'll take things quietly for a day or two, until I settle in. Thanks anyway.'

Michaela shrugged one shoulder good-naturedly. 'Well, you know you're always welcome to join us.'

With these words she swept up her car keys, which were sitting on the table by the front door, and let herself out. Tim removed his helmet and swung off the bike with an easy, athletic movement, unzipping his leather jacket as Michaela strolled over to him. Sonia watched her tip her head back in laughter at something he said. She tossed him the car keys, which he caught deftly. They were still laughing as they climbed into the car. It reversed with a roar, to spring forwards down the gravel drive.

At that moment, an unfamiliar figure rounded the corner of the house from the direction of the kitchen. He was about fifty, with hands thrust into the pockets of his shabby jeans, the sleeves of his jumper pushed up to reveal knotty forearms. A large, hound-like dog ran ahead of him, sniffing the undergrowth.

Suddenly the man stopped, catching sight of Sonia. His face registered incredulity, but snapped round as Lewis's car came into view. Whistling to his dog, he disappeared into the trees.

Sonia watched Lewis approaching the door, appreciating his lithe body beneath the formal suit. *Don't*, she chided herself as he entered the hallway. 'Lewis, who was that man? He looked very furtive.'

A flicker of annoyance crossed his

features. 'That was Harry Neill. He knows he shouldn't be in the grounds — he's trespassing.'

'But who is he?'

'He rents the only one of the three labourers' cottages that's still intact, down past the river. He used to do some gardening and odd-job work here, but we couldn't afford to keep him on. He was never very pleasant, but once we let him go, he became quite offensive. He does labouring work round about. We let him keep renting the cottage, but he seems to think that gives him the right to walk his dog through our grounds.'

'I thought he looked a bit taken aback when he saw me. He must have thought everyone had gone out.'

'It's that red hair. He maybe thought he was seeing things.'

Sonia turned away, wishing again that she had never coloured her hair. It was now another barrier between herself and Lewis.

'Look, Sonia . . . I was wondering if

you would mind doing something for me . . . When you feel like it, of course.'

Relieved at his dismissal of her resemblance to Juliette, she looked up at him. 'What is it?' It was unlike Lewis to be so hesitant.

'This may be hard for you . . . but I was wondering if you would go through Juliette's things . . . you know, her clothes, jewellery, make-up. Your grandmother isn't up to it, and Michaela wasn't that close to her. I feel it would be much better for all of us if they could be sorted out, and we could decide what to keep for Kirsty.'

Sonia nodded. 'It must be hard for you, seeing them every day in your room.'

He looked surprised at her comment. 'But didn't you realise? I don't use that room. I sleep in the smaller bedroom across the corridor.'

'Oh, I see.' Though it had been a natural mistake to make, she hoped he wouldn't think her foolish. With a small surge of hope, she wondered if that had been the situation when her cousin was still alive. 'Then I can go in anytime?'

'Whenever you feel you can face it. I'm sorry, I know it's a difficult thing to ask.'

'Of course I'll do it.'

'Thanks.' He smiled, and it was the first time she had really seen the coldness disappear from his face. But before she had time to register more than a flip of emotion, he had turned from her and walked towards his study.

Her grandmother was waiting for her at quarter past four, immaculate in her pale blue coat, with matching hat and gloves. Sitting in the hallway on a tapestry-covered chair, she looked like a picture of a bygone age.

Felicity nodded with approval at Sonia's floral skirt and cream jacket. 'Very pretty, dear. Are you ready to go now?'

'Yes, but you'll have to direct me. I've never driven up to the cathedral before.'

Felicity had a disabled parking badge, so they were able to park by the

Palace Green in front of the cathedral. Entering the quadrangle at the corner opposite the great church, Sonia was struck anew at the impressive scale of the solid Norman cathedral. It was a beautiful setting, with the small castle on the other side of the green. This had once been home to the Prince Bishops, but now housed some of the university students.

Sonia guided Felicity along the path to the massive entrance door of the cathedral. They approached the fierce lion face of the sanctuary knocker, once a haven to those fleeing from the law. This was a replica, the original now housed in the crypt museum. The entrance thronged with tourists, as well as those who had come for the service.

Once evensong was over, Sonia and her grandmother sat unmoving while the other members of the congregation departed. Eventually the church was left to the tourists, wandering in the shadows of the massive pillars beyond their vision.

Felicity had closed her eyes. Suspecting that she was praying, Sonia stayed silent.

'Sonia, dear.' Felicity reached for her granddaughter's hand. 'You did a very kind thing, coming back to see Juliette. What she did was very cruel.'

'Oh, Granny, I couldn't say that kindness motivated me. But I felt I had to make a start somewhere. My life couldn't go forward until I had faced her.'

Felicity patted her hand. 'That was very brave of you. But I could see that Juliette was very sorry about what happened. I saw a difference in her after your accident. I knew she wouldn't have the courage to contact you, so that's why I asked you to come.'

'And were you really unaware that I *was* coming?'

'Yes, there was a lot of post that we didn't open after she died. I believe Lewis found your letter this week when he finally went through everything.'

'You don't think . . . that it was one

of the things that contributed to . . . to what she did?'

Felicity looked up quickly. 'Her suicide, you mean?'

'Yes . . . '

Felicity turned her head suddenly, looking for a few moments back down the nave before facing Sonia again. Her grip was surprisingly strong. 'I needed you to come here with me today, because I don't believe Juliette would ever have taken her own life. If you'd seen her, the few weeks before, she was so full of life. She never stopped singing . . . her wonderful voice.' Felicity faltered at these words.

'Granny, what are you trying to tell me?'

The faded blue eyes looked at her steadily, as if assessing whether or not she should continue. Finally she said, 'I think someone killed her.'

Sonia snatched away her hands, pressing them against her cheeks, gasping.

'I know it's a terrible thing to say,' Felicity continued. 'But that girl seemed happier than she'd been in years. Their marriage was over, we were all aware of that — save the little one, of course.'

'But what . . . ?'

'She was leaving him. She never mentioned anything to me, but that's what the note said — not that she was going to kill herself.'

'Granny, think what you're saying. Why would anyone kill her? Do . . . do you know who?'

'No, of course I don't. It could have been a vagrant, a robber. But I just know she wouldn't commit suicide.'

'Everyone assumed that, because of her mother . . . '

Felicity sighed. 'Kathleen was a totally different character. Juliette took after her father rather than her mother. You know what Paul was like — confident, attractive — and he manipulated people for his own benefit. Kathleen needed a strong personality like that to direct her life. She drifted without him. Life had no meaning at all for her when he died — and Juliette couldn't fill the gap. It was a hard thing for a sixteen-year-old girl to face, but she had her father's strength. She wouldn't take that way out.'

Sonia's thoughts went back to that time. She remembered little about Juliette's reactions, even though they had both lost their fathers at the same time. Paul had been a keen mountaineer, and Aidan, too, before he was married. It had always been Paul's ambition to climb Mont Blanc, and when one of the climbers had pulled out of the expedition he'd organised, he persuaded Aidan to join him. They never came back. Teresa, his wife, knew that Aidan hadn't really wanted to go. But when Paul had turned on the charm his twin couldn't resist.

Born together, died together. Looking back on it after years of healing, it had seemed a fitting end. But Paul's wife, Kathleen, had never healed. It had been a bleak time for all the family. Teresa had never openly accused Paul of causing his brother's death, but she had remained cool. Maybe this had contributed to Kathleen Landale's sense of isolation, and ultimate suicide. But whatever the reason, she had taken an overdose of sleeping pills barely three years after the brothers lost their lives. Juliette was an orphan at sixteen. And now she was dead, too.

'Granny . . . Do you think it could have been someone we know?'

Felicity shook her head. 'I just don't know, dear. But I feel . . . We ought to try and find out something. I hope we'll discover that it was a stranger. There must be some sort of evidence.'

'But I haven't the slightest idea where to start. Shouldn't we go to the police?'

'As far as they're concerned, it's a closed case — suicide. It's going to be up to you, Sonia.

Sonia couldn't bring herself to believe that her grandmother's suspicions were any more than wishful thinking. It was heartbreaking to believe that her cousin had committed suicide, leaving her family wracked with guilt. But it was even more terrifying to think that she might have been murdered. And how could Sonia discover the truth?

While she thought about what she should do, she decided to give herself time to get to know the area again. But she soon found herself caught up in everyday concerns. The half-term break was over, and Kirsty had returned to school. The nanny had always collected her from school, but now there was no-one to look after her. So Sonia volunteered to pick her up after school. Mrs. Howe was happy to provide the child with her tea before leaving for the day.

On the Monday, Lewis arrived home early enough to play a game with her, then bathed her and put her to bed. But on Tuesday, work detained him at the office. Sonia took the call.

'Was that Daddy?' came a small voice from the kitchen door. Kirsty stood cuddling her kitten, eyes huge with disappointment. 'Isn't he coming home yet?'

Sonia smiled ruefully. 'No, he's got to work tonight.'

There was a pause. 'Auntie Sonia, will you play with me? I have to give Mitten her food, but maybe we could take her into the garden until Daddy gets home.'

The little face was so alight with hope that Sonia put aside any fears that she would prove inadequate at child care. 'Of course I will. Come on.' She held out her hand, which was grasped eagerly.

So began a pattern for the week. If Lewis didn't arrive home in time, Sonia would play with Kirsty. She discovered again the joy of the colourful children's books, reading them to her rapt charge. They made jigsaws, played board games, dressed dolls, played with Mitten, and Sonia found she was enjoying herself as much as Kirsty. On Thursday Lewis didn't even arrive before his daughter's bedtime, so Sonia bathed her and put her to bed, staying in the room until her eyes grew heavy and she dropped into sleep, hugging the worn, one-eyed rabbit.

She was leaving Kirsty's room when Lewis appeared in the corridor, still in his coat.

'So Kirsty's asleep?' he asked. When Sonia nodded, he sighed. 'I'm sorry. I just couldn't get away.'

Sonia smiled. 'It's all right, she wasn't any trouble. She understands that you have to work late sometimes.'

'Has she . . . ever mentioned Juliette?'

'No — just the first time she saw me. She wondered if her mother had come with me.'

Lewis frowned, rubbing his forehead with one hand. He said nothing, but walked back to the main part of the house. It was as if he had forgotten her existence completely. Something seemed to be troubling him, but if she were to question him, she knew she risked being snapped at. Despondently, she felt as if a vast ravine seemed to stretch between them.

The following morning, Sonia decided that it would be better to begin looking through Juliette's belongings while she still felt stunned, rather than when the real loss sank in. The bedroom looked cool and unused. She should have noticed it before, she thought, when she had been looking for the music score for Laura.

Sonia surveyed the room for a few moments, wondering where to start. Finally, she chose the wardrobe. Reaching forward to slide the door to one side, she found that something was jamming the door. Luckily it wasn't heavy, so she managed to push it further back to make room for the door to open.

The obstruction turned out to be a large suitcase. It certainly hadn't been there the last time she looked in the wardrobe. There were a lot more clothes hanging up, too. She reached forward to touch a black evening dress. That hadn't been there before, nor had the green velvet, or that midnight-blue silky sheath.

Her heart beating rapidly, Sonia stepped back from the wardrobe. After a pause, she began pulling open drawers. Her suspicions were confirmed — they were full now, not half-empty.

For a moment she wondered if Michaela was using the wardrobe space, but a quick check confirmed that the evening dresses were in Juliette's size. Michaela was small, like Sonia, and had the same light build. Juliette had always been taller, and took a size larger in clothes.

Sonia sat on the bed, trying to make sense of her findings. Why should Juliette's clothes have suddenly appeared in the room? They must have been in that suitcase, which implied that Juliette herself had packed a case. Why would she take her clothes if she was going to kill herself? And more to the point, who had returned the clothes and the suitcase?

Felicity was right. Juliette didn't think she was going to die. *She was murdered.*

This, surely, was evidence — and what was more, evidence that whoever killed Juliette had had access to her bedroom.

Pushing the drawers back with shaking hands, another thought struck

Sonia. Someone had seen Juliette's note before the police, and had decided that it would be read as a suicide note — and that same person had had plenty of opportunity to replace the suitcase and the clothes in Juliette's room.

Lewis.

It must be him. He had the motive, and the opportunity. Sick at heart, Sonia fled to her own room, unable to face any more. Why did it have to be Lewis?

5

It was a few days before Sonia had the heart to return to clearing Juliette's belongings. Even then it was hard, as if she was parcelling up the memories of her cousin when she was selecting what was to go to charity shops and what to keep. Opening Juliette's stage make-up box, the smell brought recollections of her own performing days flooding back. All at once she was in a crowded theatre dressing room, dancers all round her, changing into tights and costumes, fastening satin shoes with ribbons.

Sonia snapped it shut, breathing quickly. She wasn't going down that road. Still, she couldn't throw it away. The stage had been important to Juliette, too. This was something to keep for Kirsty to remember her mother by. The jewellery box was next. Flipping open the lid, she found a jumble of earrings, bracelets and necklaces. Many were paste, worn on the stage, but there were a few good items. Sonia had the idea that something was missing, though she couldn't think what it could be. Locking the jewellery box, she left it in the top drawer of the dressing table. These would all be Kirsty's when she was older.

Sonia had telephoned her mother to tell her that she was staying indefinitely because of the situation with the house. But now she had to find some work. Until something turned up she decided to hone her skills. On Saturday morning she went to see Lewis.

'Kirsty will have to go to Nicola's on Monday afternoon. I've signed up for a course in Durham.'

Lewis looked surprised. 'So what will you be doing?'

'I did some qualifications in office skills last year in Canada and I'm going to a refresher course at a private secretarial college in Durham.'

'So it's just on Mondays?'

'All day Monday, and Tuesday

morning. It'll last until the end of July. I'll still be able to drop Kirsty off at school on my way in.'

'I had no idea that you had secretarial skills . . . Funnily enough, Bill and I are looking for a part-time typist at the moment. One of the girls is leaving to have a baby next month. It's only two days a week. Would you be interested?'

Taken aback, Sonia paused for a moment. She hadn't expected the offer of work so soon, or to be working for Lewis. Still, the money would be useful. 'Yes, I would like the work. Of course, I'll have to look for a full-time job eventually.'

'That's fine with me. As long as you give us plenty of notice if you want to leave.'

'Don't you want to test my skills?' she asked mischievously.

Lewis laughed. 'Well, you can come in on Wednesday morning if you like, to give us a demonstration. But I'm sure you'll make the grade.'

Sonia left the study, still smiling. Then she frowned. Oh, this was so hard. Sometimes she forgot the real reason why she was staying, and that Lewis was the main suspect for Juliette's murder. It would make her task so much easier if he were a complete stranger — although sometimes, when he was cool with her, it seemed as if he was unknown to her.

Basically, she didn't really know where to start to look for proof. Granny had said just to keep her eyes open. But she'd been doing that for two weeks now, and everything seemed to be completely normal — except for the clothes. And if Lewis wasn't the culprit, then who could it be?

'You're looking very serious, Sonia.'

Startled by Michaela's voice, she swung round guiltily, as if her thoughts were clearly to be read. 'Oh, it's nothing. Lewis has just offered me some secretarial work at the practice and I hadn't expected that.'

Michaela raised her eyebrows. 'Well,

that's certainly a surprise to me. I can't imagine you doing a humdrum task like typing. I hated it when Michael got me the job in the local government offices. Finding the art gallery was bliss.' Felicity and her husband had been like parents to her, and it was natural that her uncle would put in a good word for her where he could. But Sonia had to agree that she could never imagine Michaela in an office.

'Well, I have to earn some money. The job is sitting down, which is the main thing — I can't do anything very active at the moment. I don't know if I ever will.'

Michaela reached out to squeeze Sonia's arm. 'I'm sorry. I didn't mean to drag all that up. It must be so hard for you. I expect you miss the ballet very much.'

Sonia sighed. 'I do, almost all the time. That's one reason why I want to start work, so that I can be busy. I'm beginning a refresher course on Monday.'

'Well, I've got some news that ought

to cheer you up. I bumped into Laura Kendall in Alderburn, and I've invited her over for supper tonight.'

Remembering Bill Kendall's daughter, and her search for the Tchaikovsky score, Sonia felt an unaccountable pang of antagonism. 'Yes, we did meet.'

'She used to come over here quite often before . . . Well, I thought it would be nice to pick up the friendship again. She's much the same age as you, which is nice. I've invited Tim, too. We rather like dressing up for these little parties, so I hope you've got something pretty. Drinks at seven thirty. Ciao!' With a wave of her hand, Michaela swept out of the front door.

It seemed as if something unexpected turned up to disturb her everywhere she turned. Sonia's clothes were still on their way from Canada, but she managed to find a short floral summer dress with thin straps that looked quite pretty. She pinned up her hair and applied some make-up for the first time in weeks. Surveying herself in the mirror she didn't think she looked too bad, but she had a feeling that Laura would outshine her without any trouble.

Making her way downstairs, she heard a voice calling her.

'Sonia! How nice to see you again.'

Sonia's amazement at seeing Laura on the landing above must have shown in her face, as their guest hurried down to take her arm.

'Oh, don't mind me. I'm a familiar visitor, and I've been up to see your grandmother. She and I have become quite friendly since I became a next-door neighbour.'

Laura certainly seemed to know her way around, Sonia thought with a stab of resentment. Their guest may well have disturbed Felicity when she was resting. Not only was she hijacking Lewis, but now her grandmother as well. Only politeness prevented her from challenging Laura.

'Ah, I see you two have met up again.' Michaela came over to greet them, glass in hand. 'Tim's doing the honours with the drinks. What'll you have, Laura?'

Glancing over to the sideboard, Sonia could see that Tim looked perfectly at home, too. At that moment his eyes caught hers. He gave her a long, appreciative look, nodding his head approvingly, with a small quirk of the lips. Taken off her guard, Sonia felt herself blushing and looked away quickly.

Tim seemed to have taken over Lewis's place, serving the drinks. He was standing by the window, pensively sipping a gin and tonic. She remembered from the past that Lewis hated dinner parties. He preferred the quiet of his own family. It had been a constant source of irritation to Juliette. Noticing Sonia, he now came to join her, smiling.

'That looks pretty, Sonia.'

Warmth flooded her at his genuine appreciation. 'Thanks — it was all I could find that would be suitable.'

Laura joined them, drink in hand. 'I

forgot to ask, Sonia. Did you find my music score?'

'The Tchaikovsky? No. I had a good look, but it hasn't turned up.'

'What is it you've lost, Laura?' Michaela handed Sonia her drink.

'It's an opera score, by Tchaikovsky, *Eugene Onegin*. I wanted to borrow it for an audition, which is next month. Sonia couldn't find it.'

'Why, all Juliette's music is in the music room. I'll find it for you.' She swept out of the room, heedless of Sonia's protests that she had already looked there.

A few moments later, Michaela returned. 'There you are, Laura. *Eugene Onegin*.'

'Oh, thanks Michaela. That saves me some needless expense.'

'But . . . I don't understand. It wasn't there when I looked.'

Michaela patted Sonia's shoulder. 'It had been pushed towards the back, that was all. I'm very good at finding things.' She laughed, picking up her glass again, and took Laura over to Tim.

Sonia frowned. She was certain the score hadn't been on the shelves. She had searched thoroughly after Laura had asked for it. Like the clothes, someone must have replaced it.

After supper they took coffee in the music room. Laura played the piano and sang for them, and, while everyone's attention was on her, Sonia moved to the shelves to look more closely. Was it her imagination, or did the scores look more tightly packed than before? Had someone replaced these as well? She didn't know what to think any more.

Later that week Sonia went into Lewis's office, where Bill Kendall gave her an informal interview, then a senior secretary gave her a skills test. Reporting that she had passed with flying colours, Bill told her they would be happy for her to start when Emma left.

When she returned home she found Tim lounging in one of the seats in the music room, reading a motorbike magazine. He looked up with a grin when he saw her.

'Hello, Sonia. Have you seen Michaela out there?'

Sonia stopped by the door. 'No, I've just come in. I thought she was at the gallery.'

Tim tossed the magazine onto a low table at his side. 'We collected the invitations for the preview to my show and we've been doing a few personal deliveries. It looks better rolling up in a smart sports car rather than on a bike!' He jumped to his feet. 'That reminds me, I've got yours here. I wanted to give it to you myself.' He gave her a roguish look.

Flustered at his unwanted flirtation, Sonia could only say, 'Oh, thanks. Of course I'll be interested in coming. When is it?'

'Next Wednesday.' He handed over a pale blue envelope. Inside was a deckle-edged card, with a cartoon of Tim in traditional artist's garb of smock and beret, a dripping brush in one hand. The caricatured grin was wider than ever.

Sonia gave a chuckle. 'I like the cartoon.'

'A sample of our dear Tim's talents.' Michaela's amused voice came from the doorway. 'But it's not all as frivolous. It'll be a good show. I hope you'll come, Sonia.'

'Yes, of course.'

'I'm ready now, Tim.' She turned to Sonia, explaining. 'Silly of me, I spilt a cup of coffee on my suit at lunchtime. We'll drop it off at the dry-cleaner's on our way through the village.'

Tim retrieved his magazine, stuffing it into one pocket of his leather jacket. 'See you Wednesday, Sonia,' he called as they exited together. Michaela took his arm to usher him through the door ahead of her. As ever, Sonia wondered about their relationship. But she was sure she had read frank admiration in his eyes, and recently she'd felt as if he were mentally undressing her every time he looked at her. It was a puzzle, like so many things at Alderburn Hall.

Sonia was curious to see Tim's work,

and wasn't disappointed by the preview. There were only about ten people at the gallery when she arrived, and the only two she recognised were Tim and Michaela. Two waitresses in black skirts and white blouses poured wine and offered canapés to the guests. Accepting a glass of wine and a biscuit topped with a sliver of Brie, Sonia wandered through the exhibition with her catalogue. Each picture had merely a title and a date beside its number.

It was active stuff, each one showing figures engaged in some energetic pursuit. There were surfers, athletes, team sports, and the inevitable motorbikes. They weren't strictly representational, but were full of colour and motion. Sonia was impressed. She paused in front of a painting of two dancers in practice gear. He'd portrayed the lines and momentum admirably as they leapt across the picture.

'I thought I'd find you here. What's your expert opinion?'

Tim stood at her shoulder, unusually

smart in a jacket and trousers with an open-necked silk shirt. He took a gulp of his wine.

Sonia nodded. 'I like it. They look really . . . alive. Like all your exhibits.'

'Thinking of buying it? A red spot would look rather fetching.' His eyes twinkled.

She shrugged ruefully. 'My pockets — and my bank balance — are empty, I'm afraid.'

'I'll tell you what . . . ' He leaned forward, putting his free arm round her shoulder. 'If it's still unsold at the end of the evening, I'll make you a present of it.'

She stepped back, finding his touch disturbing. 'But Tim, I couldn't . . . It must be worth a lot.'

'Five hundred pounds, to be precise. A snip!'

'It's no joking matter! That's a lot of money for a young artist.'

He was suddenly serious, one hand reaching out slowly to touch her hair. 'For Juliette's cousin . . . anything.'

At that, he turned on his heel, and made his way towards the door, where more guests were arriving. Sonia felt her heart pounding. What had he meant by that? What did Juliette have to do with anything? Suddenly feeling oppressed by her conflicting emotions, she laid her half-empty glass on the nearest window-sill. While Tim and Michaela's attention was taken by the new arrivals, she slipped past them into the street.

She walked towards the Framwellgate Bridge. The evening was warm, and the river Wear moved slowly beneath her. Leaning on the parapet, she gazed up towards the cathedral, lit by spotlights in the dusk. Groups of young people wandered over the bridge, their voices muted, peppered with occasional bursts of laughter.

Juliette and her friends had often congregated here during the summer months, with Sonia an eager hanger-on. With a pang, she realised that she missed her cousin very much. Even though the older girl had been less than chummy when her cousin had been her alibi, she had been eager to confide in her when they reached home.

Tearing herself away from her memories, she walked back to where she had parked her car. She really ought to put the past from her mind, before it overwhelmed her with sadness.

The exhibition ran for three weeks. In that time she saw little of Michaela or Tim. When she wasn't at her course, she was involved with Kirsty, and also started work at Lewis's practice. They arranged for her to work three days until half past two, rather than two full days, so that she would be able to collect the little girl from school.

Lewis was very apologetic about relying on Sonia so much for looking after his daughter.

'I'm glad to help,' Sonia reassured him. 'Kirsty likes me, and it's rather nice for me to have her company. She's no trouble at all.'

'But you will let me know if it interferes with anything you want to do.

I don't want you to feel that you're an unpaid nanny. I really must contact an agency.'

'No, don't do that yet. She's had enough upsets in her life recently. Anyway, she doesn't need a proper nanny, just someone to be with her after school. I'm quite happy to do that for just now.'

'Well, as long as you don't mind . . . '

She smiled. 'Don't worry.' She felt happier as Lewis seemed to be softening in his attitude towards her. *But keep your distance*, she warned herself, as the thought of her suspicions crept into her mind. She tore her gaze away from him, not wanting him to discern her feelings.

That weekend, she returned late from a shopping expedition, buying some smart, practical clothes for work. Throwing the bags on the bed, she was surprised to see a large parcel wrapped in brown paper, propped against her dressing table. Ripping off the paper, her suspicions were confirmed. It was the painting of the dancers.

A scrawled card lay on the dressing table. 'Sorry I missed you. Have lunch with me tomorrow? You owe me that at least. T.'

Still holding the card, she sank onto the bed. More complications. Luckily the paper wasn't too torn, so she was able to slip the painting back inside its wrapper. Leaving her shopping untouched, she carried the picture back downstairs. She couldn't possibly accept it.

'Have you bought a painting?'

'Oh, Lewis, this is very embarrassing. I admired it at Tim's exhibition, and he said he would make a gift of it to me. I thought he was joking — but I found it in my room today when I got home.'

'May I look at it?'

'Of course.'

Lewis slid it from the paper and studied it intently. 'Yes, it is good. Full of energy.'

'Did you get to the show?'

He shook his head. 'I meant to, but with one thing and another, it was the least of my priorities. I didn't realise he was so talented.'

'Tim wants to take me out to lunch tomorrow. I'll insist that he takes it back then.'

Lewis gave her a sharp look, strange and solemn. After a slight pause, he spoke. 'Well, that'll be nice for you.'

'You think I'm muscling in on Michaela's patch?'

He shrugged. 'I don't quite know what's going on there. I suppose he's just her protégé.'

'I feel it's the least I can do, to accept his invitation.' Suddenly she thought: *why am I justifying myself? I have every right to go out with Tim if he asks me.* She decided to talk it over with her grandmother.

It always seemed so peaceful in Felicity's room. The old lady welcomed her when she knocked, putting down the magazine she had been reading.

Sonia explained about the painting, and Tim's invitation. 'What do you think, Granny? Is there something between Michaela and Tim?'

Felicity smiled and patted her granddaughter's hand. 'I don't think you have to worry about hurting Michaela's feelings. I'm sure she'll be pleased for you two to be making friends. She's said before she wishes Tim had more friends his own age.'

'But they seem very close,' Sonia said, frowning.

'Don't worry. Just enjoy yourself. You deserve to have some fun, too.'

'But what about the painting? I can't possibly accept it!'

'Discuss it with Tim tomorrow. After all, it's his to bestow as he thinks fit. I believe he's done very well from the exhibition.'

'All right — if you think so.'

Michaela did seem pleased that Tim was taking her out, wishing them both a good time as they left. She even lent them her car, though Sonia had protested that she could quite easily take her own.

Tim drove with ease; the windows were down to let the wind blow through their hair. As they hurtled down the country lanes, Sonia wondered if it had been Tim or Michaela who had been driving the red car that had almost mown her down on the day she had arrived at Alderburn. He certainly liked speed. She watched him surreptitiously while he drove.

Tim was a good-looking man, she acknowledged. His skin glowed with a healthy tan built up over years of outdoor pursuits. Today he was wearing a linen jacket over the inevitable T-shirt, and faded but freshly washed jeans. Noticing her scrutiny, he turned to her with a smile.

'What are you thinking?'

She laughed. 'I was just wondering who does your laundry.'

His grin widened. 'I thought you were going to tell me what a fine figure of a man I cut. Well, if you must know, I can manage a washing machine perfectly well, and I'm quite nifty with an iron, too. It must be all those years as a beach bum. I lived with four other guys, and there were no women around to do the chores.'

'Was that before you became an artist?'

'Yeah, I messed around for years until I decided what I wanted to do. I suppose I was a bit of a tearaway until I went to college, and I didn't improve much then. Maybe it was something to do with being adopted.'

'Why's that?'

He braked suddenly as they plunged into a leafy dip, then accelerated swiftly up the other side. 'Oh, I don't know. I guess it was a real shock when my dad told me. I was sixteen, and up till then I'd thought they were my real mum and dad. I felt as if I'd been living a lie for all those years, and didn't belong to anyone. I just went out and tried to discover who I was for myself. Stupid, really — they were good to me. But I wish I'd known when I was younger. It's hard adjusting to something like that when you're almost grown.'

'And you discovered that you were an artist.'

He gave her a swift look with another flash of a smile. 'Yeah, but it took some time.'

He slewed round a corner briskly, then pulled into a pub car park. He led her through to a smart new restaurant attached to the old building. Once they had ordered, Sonia resumed their conversation. 'So were you successful in Australia?'

'I did a college course, but when I finished I was still restless. My adoptive parents took me out there when I was a baby, so I decided I wanted to see the country where I was born. To find my roots, if you like.'

'So you must like it here, as you've stayed.'

'Yes, I've been here for nearly two years now. I messed around in London for a while — everyone goes there, as they don't know much about anywhere else. Then I came up north, saw Northumberland and Durham, and was hooked.'

'And you met Michaela.'

He seemed almost to frown at her words. 'What do you mean?' His attitude looked suspicious.

'I mean, she offered you the exhibition, at the gallery.'

His face cleared, and he smiled once more. 'Oh, yeah, that was a great break. She sort of took me under her wing, which was really nice of her.'

'So you like her.'

'Of course! She's been great. I couldn't have done it without her.'

Their food arrived at that moment, which interrupted their conversation. He hadn't given a hint of his real feelings for Michaela. Maybe she was just a sort of mentor after all. But it seemed a little out of character for her to take a stranger under her wing. Maybe there was something a little sexual on her side, being squired by a good-looking young man giving her a fillip of excitement.

'The show was a real success,' Tim announced as they began to eat. 'I couldn't believe how much money I made — I've never been so well off. It means I can stay here for another year, though I'll have to get going with the paintbrush again.'

'The painting of the dancers — I can't accept it, Tim. It's worth too much.'

He waved his fork at her dismissively. 'Rubbish. If you're that bothered about it, I'll do another similar painting for my next exhibition. Just be proud to own a Tim Warren,' he added with a twinkle.

'Well, if you really insist . . . '

He gave a mischievous smile. 'I tell you what. In payment, why don't you model for me? You were a dancer — it could be really great.'

'Oh, but I don't . . . '

'Look, come and see the studio after lunch. You can give me your opinion on my latest work, too.'

'All right, then.' She had to admit that she was curious — and she couldn't deny that he had a magnetism that wasn't unattractive. Maybe it would be better to cultivate this and try to forget Lewis.

He drove them into Durham after lunch, parking outside a Victorian house.

'My studio's on the top floor.' When he opened the door to the flat and ushered Sonia in, she gave a gasp of pleasant surprise. Stained glass fanlights in the sloping ceiling illuminated a small hallway, and large plants lined the walls. Tim led her into the main room, which took most of the space.

Like the hallway it was filled with light, but this was clear and bright. One corner was partitioned off with a screen, but the rest was obviously his studio. There was an easel in one corner, displaying another of his action paintings. This time it depicted ice-hockey players.

'I felt inspired to do it once I knew the exhibition was going well. What do you think?'

'You get so much movement into your paintings. It's amazing.'

Sonia wandered over to the large

table under the main window. It was scattered with sketches.

'Let me get you a coffee.'

'Thanks.'

She examined the drawings one by one. They were mostly of skaters, for the current painting. Each stroke was bold, like the paintings. She was so engrossed she didn't hear him return until he put the tray down on the table.

He came to her shoulder. Leaning forward, he took a sketch from her fingers and laid it on the table, before swinging her round to face him. With no further words, he pulled her swiftly to him and kissed her fiercely.

Sonia felt as if the breath had been knocked from her body. No one had kissed her quite so passionately before, and for a moment she nearly responded in kind. Then Lewis's face flashed into her mind, and she pushed Tim away.

'No . . . I can't . . . ' His actions had made her realise that there was only one man she wanted to kiss, and it wasn't Tim.

He frowned. 'I don't understand. I thought you were interested.'

'No — I'm sorry if I gave you that impression. I was just being friendly. I'd better leave — I'll get a taxi.'

'Oh, come on, Sonia. It wasn't such a big deal — just a kiss. Look, let's make up. Stay and have your coffee.'

'No. Really, it's better if I go. I can't accept your painting.' She walked to the door.

With an exclamation of annoyance, he grabbed his jacket and followed her. He unlocked the car so they could get in, and they drove back to Alderburn in silence. As they approached the house, he spoke again.

'Look, I'm really sorry, Sonia. Don't let this spoil things for us. I think you're a really great girl. I really do want you to have the painting.'

Relenting a little, Sonia turned to him. 'All right, I'll keep it if you're really sure you want me to have it.' They pulled up alongside his motorbike at the front of the hall. She leaned forward to open the car door.

His hand came swiftly to grasp hers on the door handle. 'Let me make it up to you. Let's go out somewhere next week. I promise I won't take things too far next time.'

She gave a rueful smile. 'I think we should cool down for a while, Tim. Thanks for the meal. Bye.'

She shut the car door behind her. From the corner of her eye she was aware of Tim hitting the steering wheel in frustration. He didn't follow her into the house. A few minutes later, she heard the roar of his motorcycle as he accelerated through the gates with a surge of gravel.

6

The following week, Lewis came to join Sonia in the music room, where she was reading a book. He sat in the armchair next to hers, stretching out his legs and loosening his tie. 'I skived off early today. We've got lots of things to discuss, you know. The first is that I've arranged to take Kirsty on holiday for a fortnight.'

'Oh! You mean, this weekend?' Disappointment surged through her at the thought of them going away.

'No, not for another week. Nigel Bingham, a friend of mine, is taking his family to Florida to a villa. There's enough room for the two of us to go, too.'

'That's lovely. Kirsty will be delighted.' Sonia swallowed her selfish feelings.

Lewis smiled fondly, as he usually did when talking about his daughter. 'Yes, it'll be fun for her. They have two boys a few years older than her, and their little girl is six, just a few months older than Kirsty. She doesn't know them terribly well, though they have met once or twice before she started school.'

'Have you told her yet?'

'No, I only finalised the tickets today.' He turned round to face her. 'But we'll need to start discussing a few things before I leave. I've been through a few options about the hall, and wondered if you could spare some time tomorrow evening to go over them?'

'Of course. Is there any hope of saving it?'

He shrugged. 'I think I'll need to let you see all the possibilities before I offer any suggestions.'

The following day, Lewis took Kirsty to buy some new clothes for her holiday. Sonia had taken her grand-mother for a drive, and on their return settled Felicity in the drawing room with a cup of tea. Immediately she heard the front door bang, and a small tornado whirled into the room.

'Granny! Auntie Sonia! I'm going to America to see Mickey Mouse, and Daddy's bought me some lovely clothes. Look, let me show them, Daddy. Which bag is my new nightie in? It's got Cinderella on it. And I've got *three* pairs of shorts, and two new T-shirts. What else did I get?' She delved into the bags that Lewis had dumped on the floor beside the door.

In mock agony, he limped to the settee, and threw off his trainers. 'I'm shattered! Every shop in the Metro Centre. Thank goodness we've got everything — I couldn't face going back.'

'Oh, *yes!* I've got a new swimsuit. It's pink and blue and green. Look, Granny, isn't it pretty?'

'Lovely, dear. Are you going to learn to swim when you're in America?'

A little unsure, Kirsty looked to Lewis for a reply.

'I expect so,' he said. 'But anyway, we're going to have lots of fun in the water.'

'Daddy's got some new swimming

trunks, too — and a pair of blue shorts.'

'Is nothing sacred?' He pretended to be outraged.

'We'll have a fashion parade,' Sonia said mischievously.

'Oh, no, not me. Madam here can show you everything, but mine are strictly for the Americans.' He quickly bundled his bags out of the way, while Kirsty, giggling, tried to wrest them from his hands.

'What about those lovely new red sandals?' he asked.

Diverted, Kirsty let go of the bag, and with a squeal of pleasure, opened a box. Soon she was trying on the new sandals, along with a dress in bright colours. Lewis turned to Sonia with a smile, and in that moment she felt almost as if something snapped inside her. A flush crept into her cheeks. Embarrassed at the strength of her feelings, she began talking to Kirsty, admiring her new outfit.

Sneaking a look at Lewis a few minutes later, she found him looking at her with a half-smile, his eyes warm.

Oh, Lewis, she thought, why do I have to feel this way about you? The main suspect for Juliette's murder. It would be so much simpler to fall in love with Tim. Biting her lip, she turned away.

At last Lewis persuaded Kirsty to gather the bags together and they took the purchases upstairs.

Lewis and Sonia met in the study later. She found that her heart was beating rapidly. It was all she could do to concentrate on what he was saying.

'I want to discuss with you a few developments about the hall.' He took out a folder and opened it on his desk. 'I'll run through the latest options first. The way finances stand, we're going to have to make a decision one way or another in January. These are the only possibilities, as far as I can see.' He handed her a sheet of paper, on which he had written:

1. Sell the house outright.

2. Raise the money to convert the house into apartments, then sell the individual units.

3. Sell some of the buildings or land for income.

4. Rent out some of the buildings or land for income.

'We're just managing to run the house from week to week, but there is serious work that needs doing.'

'Such as . . . ?'

'Damp in the kitchen and the drawing room, for a start. The drains regularly become blocked and could do with being replaced. The pointing is in such a poor state that the walls are beginning to crumble in some places . . . and, most seriously, the roof needs replacing. We've had small jobs done to keep going, but it can't be put off any longer. We had an appalling winter last year with the leaks. One of the attics is completely unusable.'

Sonia sighed, laying down the paper. 'So how much money would these options bring in — I mean, all those, bar selling the hall?'

'Well, if we raise money to develop the house, we would have to get a bank loan to pay for the work — and ultimately, we would only be able to live in a small part of it because we'd have to sell off most of it to pay off the loan. It could take years, and we could end up making a loss with the property market as it is.'

'Selling land?'

'Your grandfather, Michael, sold off a lot when he lost money due to bad investment. We already rent a field to Davis, the farmer. The best option would be if we could sell some land for development, but I doubt if anyone could get planning permission to build here.'

'Renting?'

'We could rent paddock space, but there's not enough to bring in a big enough income for what we need.'

'Oh, Lewis, that means we don't have any options at all except selling. What about grants?'

'I've looked into that, too. There's nothing we're eligible for.'

'Then that's it. We're going to have to sell.' It seemed a dreadful prospect, even though she hadn't lived at Alderburn for several years. In the past few weeks, it had really begun to feel like home again. Unexpectedly, tears began to fill her eyes.

Lewis leaned across and covered her hand with his own. 'Don't give up hope, yet. There's one more option.'

The shock that coursed through her as their skin touched almost blanked his words from her mind. Sonia forced herself to pay attention to what he was saying.

'Michaela came to see me a few days ago with a proposition.' He leaned back, releasing her hand. Disappointment washed over her as he was business-like again. 'She's offered to buy a share of the house, so that we hold it in three equal parts. She doesn't have all the cash, naturally, but reckons that she could raise a mortgage on her income. We would get the money to carry out essential repairs — but of course, it further divides the ownership of the house.'

'Would that be a good idea?'

'Well, we could solve that by one of us selling to her outright, if she could raise the money. It's a bit difficult for me, as I'm acting for Kirsty. Who knows if she'll want to live in a big house with huge maintenance costs once she's grown. She may want to travel the world, or even just move to another part of the country — or she might want a little place of her own. For that matter, what about you? If you marry, your husband may not want to live here. Do *you* want to live here for the rest of your life?'

'I love it here! I can't believe how attached I've become to Alderburn since returning.'

'But you may not always feel that way.'

'I know I don't want to sell my share, Lewis. If you don't want to give up Kirsty's part, then we could split it in three.'

He took back the sheet of paper, and paused before closing the file. 'I don't think we should make any decisions immediately. I think it's best if we both give it some time, and I'll check the legal implications. Wait till Kirsty and I get back from Florida.'

Relieved that she didn't have to decide immediately, Sonia smiled. 'OK. Is that everything?'

His face also relaxed into a smile. 'Come on, let's have a coffee. And there's a good film on TV tonight, due to start shortly.'

'Sounds like a good idea to me.'

They shut the door of the study on their problems. Lewis's arm brushed her back as they crossed the hallway. Savouring the flicker of electricity between them, Sonia was content to let other suspicions drift into the background. How lovely it would be if she could give rein to her growing feelings for Lewis.

7

Sonia took Kirsty to play at a friend's house that Monday. As she drove back through the rain, she thought guiltily that she ought to be doing more about her investigations. Mrs. Howe greeted her as she came back into the hall. 'You look a bit down in the dumps. I'm just about to put the kettle on for a coffee. Come and get warm in the kitchen.'

Sonia shrugged out of her jacket. 'That sounds like a good idea. It's a miserable day.' Maybe it would also give her a chance to ask a few questions, if she could steer the conversation around to Juliette.

Edna Howe soon had two mugs of steaming coffee ready. She opened a tin of shortbread, and passed it across.

'So, how are you settling back here, dear? I've hardly had a chance to talk to you properly since you arrived.'

Sonia stretched her legs out towards the Aga. 'It's been rather strange, coming back after all this time. The hall itself hasn't changed much, but it just isn't the same without Juliette.'

Mrs. Howe took a sip of coffee, frowning. 'It was a terrible business. Poor little Kirsty. I think she's only just beginning to get over it all. It was a blessing you arrived when you did.'

'I'm amazed how she's taken to me. She's a sweet little girl — but I wonder if I'm qualified to cope with any trauma she's suffered. I don't have any idea about children's grief.'

The housekeeper put her mug down on the hearth. 'Oh, your cousin was never a loving mother to that child. I know it's not my place to say so, but that young woman never did anything that wouldn't advance her own interests. Many times I've seen little Kirsty heartbroken because her mother hadn't kept a promise to be with her or take her somewhere.'

'But Juliette must have had lots of rehearsals and practices.'

'Oh, it wasn't her singing that took her away all the time — it was all the shopping and socialising. Trips to London, Edinburgh, Paris . . . she was always off somewhere.'

Sonia realised that Mrs. Howe could be a fount of information about the past few months. This could be a real breakthrough. 'So Juliette had a lot of friends round here?'

'Well, not so much round here. And I wouldn't necessarily call them friends, as I never saw the same people twice here at the house. I don't think she stayed with any of them when she went away, because I heard Mr. Gordon complaining about the hotel bills.'

So much for that line of thinking. 'What about Laura Kendall?'

Mrs Howe wiped some crumbs from her apron. 'Another flighty piece, if you ask me. She came round once or twice for a musical session with Mrs. Gordon, but I doubt if they were really friends. She started visiting your grand- mother a few months back, but I

114

believe she was more interested in Mr. Gordon. She'd always be making sheep's eyes at him.'

Sonia bit her lip, stifling an urge to laugh at the thought of Laura looking like a sheep. But she knew what Mrs. Howe meant. She had her own suspicions that Laura was throwing herself at Lewis. She just hadn't realised that it had been obvious before Juliette's death.

Sonia felt more confused than ever after this conversation. She tried listing all the people close to Juliette during her last months, and failed to find any real motive — except for Lewis. Could he really have been jealous enough to murder his wife? She desperately didn't want to find that he was the culprit. He had always seemed to her to be a kind person. But did she know him well enough to discount him as a killer?

Maybe it had been an accident. Perhaps they'd been quarrelling, and Juliette had slipped. He'd found the note and rushed after her to stop her leaving, and she'd fallen into the water.

But why would he cover it up?

She put her head in her hands. *Oh, Granny, I don't want this. Can't we leave things alone? I don't want Lewis to be a killer. I love him.*

There, she had actually admitted it! Trembling at this revelation to herself, she thought back over the years, acknowledging that she had found him attractive right from their first meeting. Had she always resented the fact that he had married Juliette?

All at once she felt that the situation was impossible. She had to leave, now. Pulling open the drawers, she began to heap her clothes on the bed. Then she sat down, her body shaking with emotion. It was no good. She couldn't run away, like she had always done in the past. Too many people relied on her. There was Granny with her horrific suspicions about Juliette's death, and Kirsty, who had come to depend on her so much. Then there was the hall . . .

Juliette had left her a hard legacy, she thought wryly.

At least Lewis would be going away at the end of the week. She would have to subdue her feelings, if possible, and ignore them so that they would disappear. How could she have let herself fall in love at a time like this?

By Saturday, Kirsty was flying high with excitement. Sonia packed her suitcase for her during the afternoon, as Lewis was doing some last-minute work at the office.

'Is that everything now, Auntie Sonia? There's still some space in the case.'

With a laugh, Sonia hugged Kirsty. 'You don't have to fill every little space, you know. Anyway, you might want to buy some things to bring home with you.'

'Ooh, yes, Daddy's going to give me some real dollars — that's America money, you know. I'll have my very own purse, and he says I can spend them on anything I want.'

Sonia suppressed a sigh at the mention of Lewis. It was going to be hard to keep out of his way today. He was hoping to be home in time to put Kirsty to bed. Briskly, she closed the case. 'Well, what shall we do now? There's an hour before tea. I expect Mitten would like to play with you for a while, as she'll miss you while you're away.'

'Auntie Sonia . . . come and see something.' Taking Sonia's hand, she dragged her into the playroom and handed her a DVD.

With a shock, she realised that it was a recording of the ballet, *Sleeping Beauty*. She had three copies of her own — it had been made by her own ballet company.

'Mummy showed it to me last year. She said you were the Lilac Fairy, and we watched you dance. Can we watch it again?'

Unable to speak for a moment, Sonia took the DVD. The crowning glory of her career. Many people thought it showed promise of a glittering future. She hadn't realised that Juliette had a copy. No — she couldn't possibly face watching it right now. 'Not today, poppet. We won't have time. But I promise you we'll look at it when you come back from holiday.'

Kirsty took the DVD meekly and put it back under the television set. 'Auntie Sonia . . . ' she began hesitantly.

'What is it?' Sonia asked.

'My friend Rebecca has ballet lessons in Durham. Could I go with her when school starts again?'

'I don't see why not. I could show you some steps to start you off when you get back from America.'

The child's face shone. 'Oh, thank you. Just wait till I tell Daddy.' Then she stopped, a little frown appearing on her forehead. 'Promise?'

Sonia's heart contracted. Kirsty must have been let down too often. She obviously didn't trust an adult's word without a promise. 'I promise,' she said, kneeling down and hugging her tightly. 'Now, I think we'd better go down and feed Mitten, before it's time for your tea.' More than ever, she felt that Kirsty needed her, as she had no other family apart from Lewis and Felicity. As the only son of older parents, his mother had died while he was at university, and his father had passed away shortly after Kirsty was born.

The thought of the ballet DVD haunted Sonia for the rest of the day. Lewis came home in time to put Kirsty to bed, but left immediately to go back to the office for another few hours. Sonia decided to read quietly in the nursery playroom, so that she would hear if Kirsty woke.

The house became quiet as her grandmother and Michaela finally went to bed. Kirsty had been asleep for over two hours, and it was past eleven o'clock. Lewis still hadn't returned. Sonia had a bath, but felt disturbed and knew she couldn't sleep yet.

Without putting on the lights in the playroom, she switched on the television with the sound down low, and began to watch the ballet. Her heart was constricted with nostalgia as she watched her old friends dancing in the beautiful fairy-tale costumes. There was Richard, her ex-boyfriend, dancing in a small group of soloists. At that time they had been very much in love — or so she had thought. Strangely, she found now that she could think of him with detachment. It was a reassuring discovery.

But then the music progressed towards her first entry, and she found her heart beating faster, her palms growing moist. The wicked fairy Carabosse had just pronounced the curse on the infant princess Aurora — and there was the Lilac Fairy, gliding in *en pointe*. After a few moments, she let out her breath in a sigh that caught on a sob. She could still remember every step. Her feet, her arms ached to perform the graceful movements. The screen grew blurred as she watched it through tears. She couldn't stop them, uncontrollable sobs welling up in her as she wept for all that she had lost, and somehow even for Juliette and her wasted talent too.

'Sonia . . . What is it, what's the matter?'

Lewis's concerned voice took her unawares, but she was unable to reply. Embarrassed, she dashed the tears away from her eyes, but they kept on coming. Now that she had started to cry, she just couldn't stop.

He knelt down beside her, and drew her gently into his arms. He was wearing an open-necked shirt, his jacket and tie discarded before he reached the nursery. His hair smelt of rain.

At that moment he became aware of the dancers on the television screen. 'Oh, Sonia, your lovely ballet. I bought that as a present for Juliette. How talented you are.'

'All gone . . . Such a waste . . . ' was all she could mumble into his shirt, which was growing wet with her tears.

'No, it won't be a waste, darling. You'll find a way to use it again, even if you can't dance as you once did. Hush, now.'

He rocked her gently, almost to the rhythm of the faint music coming from the television set. Gradually she felt herself calming, the tears drying.

She lifted her face from his chest. For a long moment their eyes held. The intensity of his gaze almost made her shiver. Then he brought his lips down on to hers, kissing her gently and slowly. There was a taste of fruit on his lips, she thought, as she gave herself up to the delight of responding to him. She lay back, Lewis bending to her as their kisses became more urgent, their breath beginning to quicken and their hearts beating faster.

'Lewis, oh, Lewis,' she murmured beneath his lips, her hands eagerly running over his back, into his hair, which they gripped as he lowered her to the floor. It seemed so right, her body crying out for him. Suddenly, Lewis sat back with a sigh of anguish. 'No, we can't. It's not right.'

Stunned, she raised herself to her knees. '*Not right?* What do you mean?'

He ran one hand through his hair, and over his face. 'I'm sorry, Sonia. I shouldn't have . . . It's been so long . . . Please forgive me.' His eyes could not meet hers.

Unable to speak, Sonia stood up and walked to the door. Then she turned to him, her voice cool. 'Kirsty's been asleep for a couple of hours, but she was so excited it took her a long time to settle. I'll see you in the morning.' Without waiting for any reply, she closed the door behind her. Resting against it, she found she was trembling.

Why wasn't it right? Because Kirsty was in the next room? Maybe he was feeling guilty about Juliette? Or maybe what he had said was brutally true — it had been a long time since he had been with a woman, and she just happened to be handy.

'Why is life so complicated?' she muttered, throwing herself onto her bed. Her mouth still tasted of his kisses. She lay still, half hoping that he would follow her into her room, explain his words, kiss away her fears. But the door remained silent and closed. Eventually she crept under the bedclothes and fell into a fitful sleep.

The insistent peeping of her alarm woke her from a deep sleep at six o'clock. Groaning, she slapped the button on top of the clock to stop the noise. In the midst of a huge yawn, she suddenly recalled the previous night. A weight like a stone descended on her. How was she going to face Lewis today?

A cool shower brought her round, and she slipped into jeans and a short-sleeved blouse before going to wake Kirsty. Sonia put the last few items in the suitcase, then took it downstairs. She settled Kirsty with her breakfast, then went back to the kitchen to fill the kettle. It had just boiled when she heard Lewis in the dining room talking to Kirsty. Taking the mug of coffee she had just made, Sonia slipped along the corridor and back upstairs. At quarter past seven, Sonia went back downstairs with Kirsty's toy rabbit.

To her relief, she found Michaela with them in the hallway. She would not have to face him on her own.

'Oh, there you are, Sonia,' she said. 'We were just wondering where you had gone.'

Avoiding Lewis's eyes, Sonia shrugged. 'I had a few things to do upstairs. Here's Rabbit, Kirsty.'

'Ooh, Mister Rabbit, you nearly missed seeing Mickey Mouse.' The child hugged the toy close. Here eyes were shining with excitement.

'Thanks, Sonia.' Lewis touched her arm lightly, half-smiling. It made her shiver.

'That's OK, Lewis. Hope you both have a great holiday.' She kept her voice light and impersonal, trying to shut out the memory of their fleeting passion last night.

They were standing just inside the front door. Lewis had already put the cases in the car. Kirsty flung herself into Sonia's arms. 'I wish you were coming too, Auntie Sonia,' she said.

Returning the hug, Sonia replied,

'I'm sure you'll have a lovely time with the Binghams. You won't miss me at all.' *Not nearly as much as I'll miss you both*, she thought as she took Kirsty's hand to walk her to the car. Suddenly she felt Lewis's hand on her arm. Turning to him, she could see him motioning her to stay for a moment, but with a brief shake of her head, she went outside after Michaela. Somehow she felt too raw to discuss the previous night's fiasco, especially in a frantic thirty-second rush before they left. It would be better to leave things to calm down over the next fortnight. By the time Lewis and Kirsty returned, she would be able to be much more rational.

. . . Or so she would like to believe.

8

The same afternoon, Felicity asked Sonia to take her to a hairdresser's appointment in Alderburn.

'Have you discovered anything yet?' Felicity asked as soon as the hall disappeared round a bend.

'I take it you mean about Juliette's death. No, Granny, I haven't. I just can't believe that anyone in the house could have had anything to do with it. And if it was someone outside, I don't see how I can discover who it was.'

'You're getting too close to Lewis. Yes, I've seen it,' she added as Sonia turned to her in protest. 'I see the way you look at him — and the way he looks at you.'

'Oh, no, surely not. He . . . he doesn't want me.' The memory of last night's kiss and his rejection of her made her feel like weeping with yearning.

The old lady turned to look at her. 'I wouldn't say that, my dear. But don't get involved, now. I don't know what's been said between the two of you . . . ?' Her granddaughter shook her head, not even knowing herself exactly what had passed between them. 'Well, we need to sort this out first. Now you can look around, ask a few questions, without the little one at your heels.'

'Oh, Granny.' Sonia found herself laughing almost in disbelief. Felicity didn't look the type to be a Miss Marple. But she certainly knew what she wanted. 'OK, I'll do my best. But I'm not really cut out for this.'

'I know.' Felicity placed a small, gnarled hand over Sonia's on the steering wheel. It felt cool and smooth on her fingers. 'But I think we owe it to Juliette, and to Kirsty, don't you?'

Sonia thought about her grandmother's wishes on the drive back to Alderburn Hall, wondering how she could set about her investigations. Finally she decided to do something she had been avoiding since her return to Durham — take a good look at the bridge where Juliette was supposed to have fallen.

Walking round the side of the hall, she took the path towards the river. She followed the gravel path until it reached the bridge, about half a mile from the house. The bridge, with its low wooden balustrade, stood about two metres above the water. The river was about five metres across here, and would have been flowing quite fast during a wet spell, but now was bubbling innocently over one or two large rocks.

Sonia leaned over the parapet, gazing into the water. It was assumed that Juliette had thrown herself into the river here and had hit her head on one of the rocks. Her body had been discovered on the riverbank amongst the reeds further down towards the bend, about twenty metres from the bridge. Looking at the scene of the tragedy didn't offer her any inspiration.

At that moment she heard a woman's laugh and saw a movement on the other side of the bridge. It was Michaela and Laura.

'Hello, Sonia! What are you doing here?' Michaela called.

'Oh, just having a brief walk before I go back to collect Granny from the hairdresser's.'

Michaela smiled. 'I'm so glad she's getting out a bit more. She's much more like herself. Laura's just walking me to the bridge.'

'Sorry I can't stop and talk — I've an appointment with a client at Hexham. I enjoyed our lunch, Michaela.' With a wave, Laura turned back to the farm.

Sonia fell into step beside Michaela to return to the hall. Knowing this was a good opportunity to introduce the subject of the night of the tragedy, she took a deep breath.

'I can't help thinking about Juliette, when I see the bridge.'

Michaela gave her a steady look. 'It does become easier, the more you do it. It helps to make new memories.'

'Michaela — what was it like, that

night? Had you been on the path recently?'

'I'd walked up to the farm three days earlier, and it was very muddy then. But that night?' She shrugged. 'I wouldn't really know. I was in London, you see.'

'In London!' No-one had mentioned this before.

'Yes, Tim had two paintings on show at a small gallery associated with ours in London, and I went down with him two days before Juliette's accident. Of course, as soon as we heard what had happened, we returned north.'

So if Michaela and Tim had been in London, that certainly ruled them out from anything to do with her cousin's death. So that already narrowed down the field — and made Lewis a more likely suspect. She shivered in disappointment.

'Are you cold? It isn't as warm as it looks, today. Perhaps you should have a hot drink before you collect Felicity.'

'Yes, yes, I shall,' Sonia said, rubbing

132

her bare arms. But it wasn't the air that was making her cold. She wished that she could run back to the house, leap into the car, and just drive away from it all. But even the car was Juliette's.

When she collected her grandmother, she challenged her with her discovery. 'Granny, you never told me that Michaela was in London on the night of Juliette's death.'

'Was she?' the old lady replied vaguely. 'I really don't remember. She comes and goes so much, you know.'

'Can you remember anything about any of the other people who were around at the time?'

'I'll need to look out my diary. I'm really too tired today. I think I'll just have a quiet supper in my room and an early night.'

A few days later, when Felicity finally managed to gather her thoughts with the help of her diary, all she could offer was the fact that Lewis had been working late at the office — alone. He'd arrived home just after eight o'clock, but it wasn't until around midnight that he'd realised that his wife was missing and had rung the police. Felicity had gone to bed with a sleeping pill as she'd been so agitated, but had woken in the morning to the news that they had found Juliette when they began searching at first light.

So that meant that Lewis had no alibi from about 5.30 when the rest of the staff had left the office — unless of course Bill Kendall had still been there. Therefore the next people to quiz would be the Kendalls.

The opportunity to question Bill Kendall came quite unexpectedly. The office junior, who usually made tea or coffee for everyone, took a day off, so the other staff took it in turns to do this job. The secretaries and typists mostly fetched their own, but Sonia volunteered to take in Bill's cup.

He was dictating into a hand-held machine when she entered, but he smiled genially and waved her over to his desk. He finished his sentence and switched off the machine with a flick of his thumb.

'Thanks, Sonia. I'm ready for that. Lucky old Lewis. He's probably eating ice cream and popcorn, and riding the fun of the fair, while I'm stuck behind this pile of papers.'

'I hope he is. He needs a break.'

Bill was suddenly serious. 'Yes, you're right. Poor man, he's had an appalling time.'

Sonia had to put her investigator's hat on, now that she had the opportunity. 'It must have been a shock for all the practice — and especially for you, being such a close neighbour to Alderburn Hall.' The more practice she had, the easier it became to drop into the conversation these seemingly casual, but leading remarks.

'Yes, you're right. My wife and I hadn't seen much of Juliette in the time before. Laura was very shaken by the whole business, being her friend.'

'So she had seen Juliette recently?'

'Oh, yes, just the night before she

. . . Well, there had been a 'do' with other people from the operatic society. A dinner, with dancing afterwards. Well, in the days after that, Laura kept saying, over and over, 'But she seemed so *happy*, Daddy, so *alive*.'

Obviously Laura and Bill had both been in the area at the time of Juliette's death. It was all the information she could hope for at the moment without giving away her motive for the questioning.

Later in the week, Bill's secretary brought some papers for Sonia to photocopy. 'I hope that Mr. Gordon enjoys his holiday with his little girl. He really needed to get away from this place.'

Sonia nodded. 'It'll be just what he needs, holidaying with children. It must have been so terrible for him, during that time. Do you remember the night of the tragedy?' She still had to confirm Lewis's exact movements for the time of her cousin's death.

'Oh, I'll never forget it. I was the last to leave, and I was surprised to see the light still on in his office. It must have been about quarter to six. I knocked and went in, asking him if he needed anything, but he just smiled — that nice, kind smile he has — and said, no thanks, he'd get something to eat later when he went home. He'd had to work late as there was a big case coming up in court later in the week, and anyway, his wife was going to be out.'

'But what about Kirsty? Who was looking after her?'

Madeleine creased her brow. 'I really don't know. Possibly the nanny — I don't know what her hours were. Maybe the little girl was somewhere else, too, and that was why he didn't want to go home on his own. I think the poor man was lonely. I hope you don't think I'm being personal, but Mrs. Gordon never seemed to be at home.'

Sonia gave a small shrug. 'She did go out a lot.' No matter how she felt about Juliette's treatment of Lewis, she knew she couldn't gossip about it.

Madeleine went on: 'Well, I'm just

glad that the publicity has died down now and everyone is getting the chance to get on with their own lives again. Will you bring back the photocopies as soon as you've finished?'

Sonia came to the conclusion that she needed to talk with Mrs. Howe again. The following day she pinned her down when she knew that Michaela would be at the gallery. It took very little to get the housekeeper interested in giving her own version of the happenings of that night.

'Well,' she began, making herself comfortable in her armchair beside the Aga, 'it was one of the stormiest nights we had had for a while. Mind you, we'd had lots of rain over the few weeks before that. The river was that high, I'd given up walking from the village. The paths were too muddy even for wellies, so my daughter Janice brought me up in the car most days, and either Mr. Gordon or Miss Michaela drove me back down.'

'Not Juliette?'

'No — we never knew where she was,

with all her gallivanting. If there was no-one around, then Mrs. Landale would give me money for a taxi home. Anyway, it was the nanny's night off, and Mr. Gordon was going to look after the little one. But something came up and he had to work late, and Miss Michaela was away in London, so he phoned me in the morning to ask if I would mind babysitting.

'I put Kirsty to bed at half past six, and went back downstairs to clear up. Mr. Gordon came in just after eight o'clock. He asked me if Mrs. Gordon had gone out, and I could only say that it looked like it, as I hadn't seen her at all. She'd been in when I arrived, doing something in her room. I thought maybe she'd left when I was reading Kirsty a story. He looked in on the child, and then rang for a taxi for me. We never realised she'd not taken the car ... not then, anyway. He didn't think about looking in the barn until later. That was when he called the police.'

Sonia was silent for a moment after Mrs. Howe had finished her story, imagining the events of the night unfolding. Distressingly, the testimony seemed to point yet again towards Lewis. Sonia pushed back her chair and stood up. 'Thanks, Mrs. Howe — I've one or two things to be getting on with now, upstairs.'

To her surprise, the housekeeper reached out and grasped her hand with her roughened fingers. It was a reassuring touch, the grip firm. 'I'm sorry, love, if I've stirred up bad memories. I haven't always been respectful of the dead, and she was your cousin, after all.'

Sonia nodded. 'Juliette wasn't always an easy person to live with — I know that as much as anyone. It helps me to piece together the events of that time. I just want to work out in my mind what actually drove her to . . . to . . . Well, maybe it'll help me to understand.'

The older woman patted Sonia's hand in comfort. 'I know, dear. We all need to understand it better. Just ask me anything, if you think I can help.'

Once Mrs. Howe had gone home, Sonia decided to explore the attics to see if her old practice room up there could be refurbished. Now that her leg was getting stronger it would be a good idea to begin exercising gently. Kirsty had seemed keen to start ballet, so it would be nice to give her an introduction. She sincerely hoped that it wasn't the room that had had the leak, which Lewis had said was unusable now. The practice room was on the north side of the house, but it had a skylight which gave it good light. Pushing open the door, she disturbed a cloud of dust, which set her coughing. Thankfully, it didn't appear to have any water damage. Some pictures covered by a dust sheet stood against the mirrors, which were layered in dust. Reaching a hand to wipe the glass, it rocked at her touch. The barre itself was coming away at its fixtures. There would have to be some work done on it to make it secure.

Curiosity getting the better of her,

she bent down to remove the dust sheet from the pictures. They were old paintings of farm animals, dark and in need of cleaning. But she gasped when she uncovered the last painting. Juliette in a dark blue velvet dress stared at her defiantly. This was what had been missing from the bedroom — the portrait that Lewis had commissioned of her when she had become so successful in her singing. It was a good likeness, the artist being someone Lewis had met in London while on business. No wonder he had stacked it away out of sight — she looked so alive, as if she were about to launch into an aria.

Just as she was moving to cover the painting again, Sonia drew her breath in sharply. There on her painted wrist, was the missing item of jewellery from the box — Juliette's beautiful diamond and ruby bracelet, a present from Lewis at the time he gained his partnership. Juliette had called it her good luck bracelet, and always wore it on stage. So where was it now?

9

While Michaela was still out, Sonia searched Lewis's and Juliette's bedrooms, but found no sign of the bracelet. She checked Kirsty's bedroom before breakfast the next morning, but yet again drew a blank. When she mentioned it to her grandmother later that day, the old lady had no idea where the bracelet could be. It would just have to remain another unanswered question for the time being.

Her investigations had covered the whereabouts of Lewis, Michaela, Tim, Mrs. Howe, and as far as she could judge, Laura Kendall, though she had no definite alibi for her that night. The only other main suspect was Harry Neill, and it would be difficult to obtain any information about him. It occurred to her that he might be willing to repair the mirror and barre in her practice room. She collared Michaela that evening.

'Didn't Harry Neill used to do odd jobs around the house when he was gardener here?'

Michaela pushed her heavy silver bracelet further up her arm, her red varnished nails delicately tapping it into place. 'Yes, he did. We kept him busy in the days when we could afford it. He can turn his hand to most things. I think he still does various jobs for Davis, the farmer on the other side of our land. Why do you ask?'

'Do you think he might do some repairs in my old practice room? The mirror needs fixing to the wall, and the barre is slack.'

Michaela raised one perfectly shaped eyebrow. 'You're going to use the room again? For dancing?'

Sonia shifted in her seat. 'I can still exercise, you know. Ballet exercises are very good for strengthening the muscles.'

'Well, by all means ask him. I'm sure he could do with the money. Of course, he's no great fan of the occupants of

Alderburn Hall. Juliette wanted him to leave the cottage so that it could be sold. Last time Lewis found him walking his dog through the grounds, Neill gave him a mouthful of abuse when he said he didn't like the animal making messes where Kirsty might be playing. He's an unpleasant man.'

'But is his work good?'

'Good enough. But have a word with Lewis first about how much to offer him. You could even ask him to negotiate for you.'

After thinking it over, Sonia opted to wait to ask Lewis what price he thought she should offer Neill. It was incredible to think that they would be home again in two days' time. She wondered how she would feel upon seeing him again. Would her feelings have calmed in the time they had been apart, or would her heart be stirred once more?

They arrived while Sonia was at church with her grandmother. Her chest felt tight when she drove back up the drive and saw Lewis's car outside the house. It wasn't just the thought of seeing him, or working out their strange relationship; she suddenly realised that she was longing to see her little cousin again. Felicity brightened visibly at the prospect of greeting the travellers. 'I can't wait to hear all about the holiday,' she said as Sonia helped her from the car.

'You may have to wait a little while, Granny. I expect they'll be very tired and suffering from jet-lag.'

They found a tanned and relaxed Lewis drinking lemonade with Michaela in the drawing room. His eyes immediately met hers, seeming to convey some intense message that she couldn't understand. The familiar sudden twist of emotion took her breath away. If only she could have met with him on her own, then she could really see his reaction to her.

Felicity greeted him with a hug, commenting on how well he looked. 'Where's the little one?'

He grinned. 'Sound asleep in bed. But she's had a wonderful time. The

Binghams were terrific. She didn't sleep much on the flight, either way — she was much too excited.'

'And you, Lewis — did you enjoy it?' Sonia asked, marvelling that her voice sounded so normal, when her heart was hammering madly.

He turned to her, and his eyes seemed to soften. 'Yes, it was good. Sheer unadulterated fun; no work, just sun and relaxation. It was good for me to see Kirsty so happy.'

She nodded, smiling, covering her feelings well. If only she could prove that he was innocent of his wife's murder. Somehow she had to discover the culprit, otherwise she could never allow herself to love him.

Kirsty was full of her trip to America, which seemed to have boosted her confidence. She talked non-stop about her new friends, Sarah, Jamie, and Ben. Lewis confided that the Bingham children had been very welcoming to an unknown and lonely child. Kirsty too had been able to make friends more easily than she had in the past. She had always been a shy child, and had been more withdrawn since Juliette's death.

It seemed to her that Lewis was quite happy to drift back into life as it had been before he went on holiday. He worked late at the office, catching up on work, so he wasn't around much. Sonia had hoped that there would be an opportunity to talk about what had happened the night before he went on holiday, but he remained pleasantly distant. Well, if he was going to be cool with her, she had better things to do than pine over someone who ignored her. She determined to put him to the back of her mind and get on with her life.

The first task was to telephone Harry Neill. He agreed to come over the next afternoon to look at the practice room. When he arrived, it crossed her mind that his heavy boots might damage the floor of the practice room, but in the end she said nothing. No doubt it had received far worse pounding in her days as a ballet student.

Neill wiped his hand across his stubble as he examined the mirror and barre. His eyes, which had been hooded and insolent when he rang the doorbell, were now virtually hidden by his frowning brows.

'It's not much of a job,' he said. 'It just needs a few screws.'

How rude he was! Sonia retorted, 'Well, the work's there if you want it. It needs to be really firm.'

'OK. How much are you offering?' He stared at her, unsmiling.

Sonia mentioned the amount Lewis had suggested, at which Neill nodded. 'Fair enough. When d'you want it done?'

'As soon as possible.'

'I can do it Monday evening. I'm helping Davis with the harvest before that.'

He arrived punctually at six thirty on the evening as arranged. Sonia let him in, and went to take him upstairs.

'No need. I know my way round this

place. They were glad enough to have my services in the past.'

'Well — all right. Do you want a cup of tea or coffee?'

'Wouldn't say no. Tea, milk, two sugars.' He disappeared up the main staircase without a backward glance.

Lewis emerged from his study. 'Was that Harry Neill?' When Sonia nodded, he added, 'I need to see him about something before he goes. Will you ask him to come to my study when he's finished?'

Sonia took the tea up, and found Neill removing the screws from the mirror and barre. He offered no thanks, merely nodded as she put the mug down. When he heard Lewis's message, he retorted crossly. 'Making trouble again about the cottage, I bet. *Madam* — ' He spoke the word with a sneer. ' — was always going on about it.'

'Do you mean my cousin, Mrs. Gordon?' Sonia said pointedly.

'Yes, she wanted to sell off my cottage. But I wouldn't move for her, and I'm not leaving it for anyone now.' He glared at Sonia defensively.

Anger surged inside her, but she curbed any retort. Now was her chance to question him, while he was talkative. 'She must have had so many worries, to do what she did.'

'Jump in the river, you mean? If she did, then she did a lot of people a favour.'

He was so unpleasant! But she had to continue with her questioning to get the information she needed. 'Why do you hate her so much?'

'Your darling cousin,' he stated, pointing a finger at her, 'never cared about anyone except herself. She could have told me where my wife and girl were — she took them away in her car when they left.'

'Oh — I didn't know.'

'Yes, always sticking her nose in, she was. But I suppose she thought I'd leave the cottage once they went. Not me. I'm staying, and nothing anyone can do will get me out.'

'So you were glad she died?'

He looked at her from the side of his eyes. 'What're you getting at? That I pushed her in? I couldn't stand her, but that's a bit much.'

'No, no, I didn't mean that.' A flicker of fear caught her at his words. She couldn't let it be known that she was hunting a murderer.

He gave a grunt, and turned back to his work. 'I'll be finished in about an hour.'

'I'll be downstairs, in the drawing room.'

Later, Sonia heard raised voices from the direction of Lewis's study. Clutching the envelope containing Harry Neill's money, she went into the hallway. At that moment the door of the study was flung open and Neill stormed out, shouting and swearing at Lewis.

'You'll never get me out, except in a coffin.' Glaring at Sonia, who was standing transfixed, he grabbed the envelope from her outstretched hand, and walked out.

The front door slammed behind him. Lewis looked apologetically at Sonia. 'I'm sorry you had to witness that.'

She shrugged. 'It's not really a surprise. Did you try to get him out of the cottage?'

'I've offered to get him a council house. I put his name down some time ago, and they contacted me today to say that one was available. I don't know why he doesn't go. The cottage is really in poor condition these days. It would make things so much easier for us, too.'

She followed him back into the office. 'Would the money from selling the cottage put the hall back on its feet?'

He shook his head regretfully. 'Nowhere near, I'm sorry to say. I just don't know what we're going to do about the hall. The sale of the cottage would just go towards death duties. I think we really are going to have to put the place on the market.'

Her heart sank. Was this going to be the end of their family home? How could she leave everyone now, especially Lewis and Kirsty? And what about Granny — where would she go? Tears began to prick at her eyes, so she turned and escaped before he could see.

10

Kirsty was fascinated by the practice room, which she had never seen before. She insisted on copying Sonia's exercises, so in the end it seemed natural to teach her the rudiments. They went to a dance shop to buy her a tiny leotard and pink ballet shoes, and they could hardly get the footwear off her feet to go to bed.

Sonia and Lewis agreed to have the hall put on the market, and he invited an estate agent to look at the property. Michaela stormed into the drawing room to confront them as soon as she heard what they proposed.

'What do you mean by putting the hall up for sale, Lewis? I can't believe you could do such a thing. And you — ' She turned on Sonia. 'What do you think you're doing? I thought you were on our side.' Her usually immaculate face was distorted into harsh lines of anger, a lock of hair falling across her forehead.

'It's all we can do,' Sonia tried to explain. 'With the death duties and its poor structural state, the authorities can take it from us and have repairs done forcibly if we don't, and we'll still be liable for the bill.'

'I don't believe you! It's our home. No-one can force us to spend money we haven't got!'

'It's true, Michaela.' Lewis stood up. 'If you come into my study, I'll go through it with you. Alderburn Hall is a listed building, and we have to keep it in a state of good repair. There's just no way we can afford it, even if you took out a mortgage.'

'You just don't want me to have a part of it! And I have as much right to it as you do!' With a last furious look at Sonia, she turned sharply and stalked back out, flinging the door shut behind her.

Sonia looked at Lewis, shocked. She had never seen Michaela so upset.

'What does she mean? How can she have as much right to it as we do?'

He frowned. 'Maybe she means that she has lived here longer than any of us — or maybe it's because she's the daughter of a younger Landale son, as you are.'

'I'd better go to her.' She levered herself up from the chair.

'No, better not now. Give her time to cool off. I'll go through things with her when she's more rational. I'm just sorry she's worked herself up so much. I never thought it would upset her so.'

Sonia agreed not to follow Michaela, but couldn't stay with him any longer. It was disappointing that their times in the study were no more than business chats. Despite many opportunities since his return from holiday, Lewis had shown no more than brotherly affection to her.

The atmosphere in the house was strained over the next few days. Michaela finally agreed to look at the figures with Lewis, but she was cool and distant with everyone except

Felicity. The old lady seemed resigned to any sale, and had little to say. She only commented that she was sure it would take some time to work out, and that she knew Sonia and Lewis would see that she had a home. Kirsty mercifully seemed unaffected by the moods of the adults, as she spent much of the week out of the house, either with school friends or with Nicola.

Sonia took the opportunity to work out gently in her practice room, feeling the ache of muscles unused for years, but finding it comforting as it reminded her of her days as a ballet student. All her exercise clothing was new, as she hadn't been able to bring herself to wear her old gear from her professional days. Somehow the clothes had made the journey to Canada and had come back to her with the other belongings that her mother had sent on. One look at the faded leotards and tights, legwarmers and sweats had filled her with misery. She had briefly pressed the soft fabric to her face, smelling the faint whiff of the fabric conditioner that her mother always used for the laundry. There was one pair of shoes that she thought she ought to keep as they were soft enough for practice. The rest went straight into the bin, before it could make her break down completely at the memory of all she had lost.

As soon as she was standing in front of the mirror again for the first time since her accident, feet in first position, she had taken a deep breath and made a *demi plié*. All at once she had entered a comforting world of moving her body in the way she had always loved. It didn't matter that she was stiff and that her bad leg wouldn't work the way it used to. It gave her something to work on, to aim to strengthen it. The constant repetitions concentrated her mind and helped her ignore the worries that threatened to invade her thoughts.

She had showered and changed after one session, and was reading a magazine in the walled garden under a tree, when she became aware of a figure watching her from the undergrowth.

Suppressing a shiver of panic, she called out, 'Who is it, who's there?'

At the sound of her voice, the watcher emerged closer to her. As his features became lit by the sunlight, she recognised Tim. With a sigh of relief, she sank back into her chair.

'You gave me a fright, skulking like that in the bushes!'

He grinned at her, flicking back a lock of curly hair. 'I hoped I'd find you.' Sprawling beside her on the lawn, he leaned on one elbow. 'I wanted to talk to you.'

Sonia laid her book down, wondering if he was going to ask her out again. She was hoping he wouldn't — she felt rude always refusing. It wasn't that she didn't like him — it was just that, no matter how much she tried to stop herself, she still felt something for Lewis.

'It's about Michaela.'

This made her sit up.

'You know she's anxious for the hall to stay in the family.'

'But we all want that! We love Alderburn Hall. Does she think we haven't tried to keep it?'

'OK, OK, don't get uptight. I just said I'd ask if you would consider her offer again. You know it's a good one.'

'Oh, Tim . . . I wish it was as simple as that. I couldn't believe it when I saw how much the repairs would cost. We're really in trouble. And to make matters worse, Lewis is the main source of income amongst all the occupants. He's fast running out of money.'

'I've got some money, too. I made nearly four thousand pounds from my last two exhibitions. I'd be willing to put in a share.'

Sonia was silent for a few seconds. 'That's very kind, Tim, but what's in it for you? It's not as if you're family.'

Tim's expression became sullen for an instant. 'Maybe not yet . . . ' he muttered.

'What do you mean?' Sonia asked sharply.

A twist of a smile graced his lips. 'Oh,

nothing. Just don't count me out completely, will you?'

Without waiting for a reply, he sprang to his feet and disappeared back the way he had come. Sonia stared after him for a while, her mind full of questions. Was Tim meaning that he was going to marry Michaela? Surely not. He always maintained that they were just friends. Or maybe he hadn't given up hope with herself. She lay back in the chair, looking at the sky. There seemed to be so many tangled threads surrounding them all. How could they be unravelled?

After thinking things over for a while, Sonia decided to confront Lewis with Tim's offer.

'Don't you think it would help to tide us over for a while? It could give us a breather just to get the authorities off our backs. I'm hoping to get some full-time work soon, and that should make finances easier.'

Lewis sighed. 'It's just not practical. That would make four of us the owners of the house. It's bad enough with two, as I tried to point out to Michaela when she offered to take a part. But as for Tim . . . well, he's not even family.'

It seemed strange that Lewis should pick on the very argument that she herself had used with Tim. But for a while this had seemed to her to be a very real way of keeping the house. Disappointment cut through her.

'I wish you'd stop being a lawyer for once,' she retorted, exasperated. 'I think this could be a real solution for us. Who cares about the legalities of it? Surely we could work out some kind of agreement.'

'I'm sorry, Sonia. It's really not a viable solution. And without my consent as Kirsty's father, it can't go forward.' His face was forbidding. 'I love this house too, but you've no idea the problems that could arise from joint ownership, especially when the people aren't related.'

'But Michaela's one of the family. What if Tim just lent her some money?'

'I just think it's all very odd. I can't help thinking there's some sort of hidden agenda.'

'Oh, you! You're so stubborn, Lewis. You should think with your heart instead of your lawyer's brain!'

Sonia stalked from his office, feeling the heat of anger burning her face. Deciding that the only way to relieve her tension was to exercise, she went to her room to change into her practice clothes. Her hands were shaking so much with the exasperation at his stubbornness, that it took her twice as long as usual to tie the ribbons of her shoes.

The practice room was quite cool as it had caught no direct sunlight that day. Almost at once her emotions began to calm. Choosing a CD, she slotted it into the machine. Slow piano music with measured beats filled the room. As Sonia turned back to the barre, she laid her hand on it ready to begin stretching. To her horror she found she was falling, still grasping the barre. As her knees hit the floor, she reached up instinctively to catch the huge mirror, which was toppling towards her.

Mercifully it didn't break. She pushed it back to the wall, shaking with the effort of taking its weight. If it had shattered, she could have been horribly disfigured, if not killed. The barre screws hung out of the wall, uselessly.

Then she found that the mirror wouldn't stay against the wall. She was stuck, holding it there. Surely someone must be in the house. Mrs. Howe or Lewis might hear her if she shouted.

'Help! Is anyone there? Can anyone hear me?' The piano music still played on from the machine. For a moment she thought she heard the sound of footsteps on the floor below. After calling a few more times, she realised that no-one could hear her — or that they were ignoring her.

How had the barre come loose so quickly? And why was the mirror no longer attached to the wall? It too should have been screwed firmly in place. Realising that she would have to do something herself, she pushed the barre away from her with one foot, and began walking away from the wall, letting the mirror come with her. She had to keep the bottom edge against the skirting board, so that it wouldn't fall to the floor suddenly and shatter. By the time she laid the top edge against the floor, her muscles were trembling from exertion.

Picking up the barre, she examined the screws. They definitely looked like the ones that she had seen Harry Neill using, and they also seemed to be good quality. In fact, there didn't seem to be any reason for the barre to fall out. But when she looked more closely at the wall, she realised that there was very little for the screws to hold on to in the plaster. Anger flared in her. He would just have to come back and re-do his shoddy work. She could have been badly injured by his incompetence!

It was only when she was halfway down the stairs to the telephone that

Sonia realised that Harry Neill said he would fill the plaster carefully, and put strong pins in the wall to hold the screws in place. She stopped abruptly, her heart pounding. If he had indeed done so, it could only mean one thing.

Someone had sabotaged the practice room with the express motive of causing her serious injury.

11

Despite her dislike of him, Sonia telephoned Harry Neill to come and repair the barre. He grumbled when he saw the state of it, but finished the work quickly. At her request, he had also brought a lock for the door. It would be disastrous if Kirsty came in while she was out, in case the same thing happened again. This time she paid him without telling Lewis about the near accident with the mirror. She didn't even mention it to her grandmother, knowing that it would only cause her anxiety.

There had been many opportunities for other people to sabotage the room while she was out, so none of her suspects could be ruled out. What was most frightening was that she herself now seemed to be a target. Had they realised that she had been making enquiries? She would have to be careful. If only she had someone other than her grandmother to confide in.

There were new puzzles for her to sort out. Why had Juliette been walking down to the village? She questioned the local taxi firms, but none had been hired to pick up her cousin in Alderburn. Possibly she had arranged to meet someone that she knew. Maybe that very person was the murderer. But the big query was: where in fact had she been going? Her next step should be to find out Juliette's movements in the weeks preceding her death. Maybe that would give her a clue.

In the meantime, day-to-day life interrupted her investigations. Kirsty was still eager to take up ballet, so Sonia arranged to take her into Durham on the first Saturday of the school term to enrol at a local ballet class. Sonia and Juliette had both been pupils there as children, before Sonia had gone away to ballet school. Miss Aldwyn, the principal, had retired a few years ago, but the school still bore her name.

The studio was above one of the shops in an area of Victorian houses just outside the centre of the city. Sonia, with Kirsty skipping excitedly at her side, followed a mother with two girls through the main door and up a steep flight of stairs to the office area. There were a few other girls with their parents in front of them, queuing to sign up for the beginners' class. Along the corridor the door to the changing room swung open, and two small girls came out hand in hand, already dressed in their pink leotards and ballet shoes. They waved to Kirsty.

'Look, that's Amy and Tania from my school.' She waved back, delighted that she had found someone she knew.

Sonia looked around and liked what she saw. The place was brighter and more inviting than in the days of Miss Aldwyn. It was now run by two younger women, called Verity and Lynn. Then, as she registered the framed photos of ballet dancers in the hall, her breath caught in her throat. There was one of herself, as the Lilac Fairy . . . and there was another, in a ballet choreographed by Richard, as Terpsichore.

Her heart began to pound. Did that mean that they would know who she was? Or were these just relics from Miss Aldwyn's days?

The mother in front of her finished her transaction and made way for Sonia. The young woman at the desk beamed a welcoming smile at them both, especially at Kirsty.

'Hello, are you joining our ballet class?'

Sonia liked her manner immediately. Kirsty nodded with a shy smile.

'Now, what's your name?'

Kirsty held back, looking to Sonia for a lead.

'Kirsty Gordon.' Sonia spoke for the little girl.

The young woman wrote the name down. 'Are you Mrs. Gordon?'

'No, I'm her . . . her auntie. But we live at the same address. I'm paying for the lessons.'

'Auntie Sonia's been teaching me in the summer holidays.'

The young woman smiled. 'Well, aren't you lucky. But you'll find it even more fun with the other girls and boys.' She held out a form for Sonia to sign, then gave her a receipt for the cheque.

'We normally stick to school terms. We tend to find it's easier . . . Oh!' she exclaimed as she read the name on the form. 'Why, you're Sonia Landale. How amazing! We've got your photos in the hall. What are you doing here?'

'Well, I thought it would be the best place for Kirsty.'

'No, I mean, I thought you were with the Southern Ballet Company.'

'I had to retire. An injury,' she said briefly. It was quite painful to say the words aloud. The young woman sensed her reluctance to talk, and rushed on, embarrassed.

'I should have recognised you. I'm Lynn Mitchell. I was in your class for a while, but you went ahead of me. Miss Aldwyn was always so proud of the fact that you had been her student.' There was a short awkward silence. 'Well . . . and now Kirsty's come to us. I do hope you'll enjoy your classes,' she said to the little girl. 'You can change along the corridor. Verity will be along shortly to begin the class.'

'Thank you.' Sonia picked up her handbag.

'It was great to see you again,' Lynn said softly. Sonia gave her a fleeting smile, and nodded. Despite Lynn's reaction, it hadn't been too bad. She took her little cousin along to change.

She was able to watch most of the lesson through the windows from the corridor, along with a few other parents. Kirsty seemed quite happy, though she looked back once or twice to make sure that Sonia was still there. But soon she would be fine on her own. Sonia was also pleased to see that Kirsty had a natural grace, and managed the movements easily. It was clear from her expression that she was enjoying herself.

Shortly before they were due to finish, she found Lynn Mitchell at her side.

'I'm sorry to interrupt you,' she said in a low voice, 'but could I possibly ask you something?'

Sonia was surprised, but nodded. She followed Lynn back to the office.

'I don't know quite how to put this . . . but I just can't let the opportunity go by.' For a moment she hesitated, as if she was having difficulty finding the right words. 'Well, let's get straight to the point. Verity and I, we hope that we run the school to the same sort of level that Miss Aldwyn did. But we do have some very talented advanced students, and we've felt for a while that we're not able to offer them the sort of teaching they deserve. What they need is inspiration from a real professional, someone like . . . well, someone like you. I don't know whether or not you'd be interested, or even if you have the time, or if . . . ' She didn't seem to know how to continue.

'If I'm physically able,' Sonia finished for her.

'Yes, well . . . you did say you'd had a bad injury.'

Sonia nodded. 'I've just started exercising again over the past few months. I'd be able to manage a few demonstrations, even though I couldn't dance professionally again.'

'Would you like some time to consider it? Take as long as you like.'

'No . . . I don't think I need time.' Sonia's face glowed as she thought of what she could do. 'I'd love to do it. I've missed dancing so much. I've been stuck in a solicitor's office since June, and I just *have* to do something more creative. When would you like me to start?'

Lynn was ecstatic. 'I can hardly believe it! Just wait till Verity hears. Just wait till the students hear. Oh, Sonia, this is going to be great. Mind you, the money's not brilliant.' She told her the rate.

'No problem,' Sonia said. 'It'll be a

pleasure. When are the classes?'

'I thought you could do two, maybe Tuesday and Thursday evening. How about coming in on Monday after lunch to discuss it with Verity and me — we have a class of tinies at half past three, so if you come at two you can have a proper look round the place. We've updated it a bit since Miss Aldwyn's days.'

'So I've noticed. I'll look forward to it.' At that moment, she heard the sound of young voices raised in the corridor as the class flooded out of the studio into the changing rooms. 'I'd better go. Kirsty will be looking for me.'

Sonia felt as if she were flying. She wanted to laugh, jump, embrace everyone with the delight that vibrated through every part of her. *I never realised how much I missed it*, she thought, feeling as if a window had been opened on her enclosed world.

Coaching the advanced students at the ballet school brought a feeling of real hope into her life for the first time since she had arrived at Alderburn. The new challenge helped her to blot out many of the worries she was harbouring. The hard shell that had built up around her began to soften and dissolve.

Felicity soon noticed the change in her. Taking her granddaughter's hand, she squeezed it happily.

'I can see you've found work which is special to you.'

'Granny, you've no idea — I think this may be what I've been looking for. I love being back in the ballet studio. You know, I never realised that I could be a teacher — but the students seem to like me. I had wondered if I would be able to teach them anything, but it seemed so easy once I'd begun. I'm so full of ideas for them!'

'I'm glad, my dear. It hasn't been easy for you. I wondered if you would stay, or try and find happiness elsewhere. But this gives me hope.'

Sonia saw the uncertainty in her grandmother's eyes, and leaned forward quickly to hug her. 'Don't worry, I won't leave you. I'll stay as long as you need me.'

'And the little one, too — she needs you.'

Sonia sat back, frowning slightly. 'Yes, I know. Kirsty's become very attached to me. I want to sort out this mystery, but . . . what if Lewis was to blame? Would we tell the police? He'd be sent away, and that would be drastic for Kirsty.'

Felicity bit her lip. 'I know, dear. I've thought about it, too. But we have to discover what really happened to Juliette, for her sake, and especially for Kirsty's sake, when she's older. So we'll find out the truth first, then decide what action to take.'

Sonia felt she had made no headway at all with her investigations. With her office job, and now the ballet coaching, there was less time to think. Then there was Kirsty's sixth birthday to organise for the end of September. Lewis wanted the occasion to be as normal as possible. Kirsty was anxious to have a party, and to invite friends from school, so they agreed to let her have her wish.

Mrs. Howe offered to cater for the party, as there were fifteen children invited. Lewis arranged for a clown to entertain the children for some time before tea, and Nicola offered to do some party games for the rest of the time. Some of the parents were a little wary at first, but relaxed when Sonia appeared to be in the place of a mother, so they could treat the set-up as normal.

Kirsty seemed to enjoy herself, though Sonia noticed that she kept looking towards the door as if expecting to see another guest arrive. Finally all the children were waved off home, clutching their 'treats', and they had the house to themselves. Kirsty played for a while with some of the gifts the children had brought.

'Well, now, young lady, I think it's time you put on your pyjamas. It's after half past eight.'

'Oh, Daddy, not yet. I can't go to bed yet.'

'I'll read you a story — two, if you hurry up. I know it's been an exciting day, but you're tired. Off you go, now.'

'No!'

Sonia started at the uncharacteristic outburst.

'Kirsty . . . '

'No, I can't go yet. Not yet, Daddy.' She began to cry noisily.

Lewis put his arm round her. 'Come on, poppet. You know it's long past your bedtime. We'll have a nice cuddle and a story . . . '

'No, Daddy! I can't go up yet, don't make me!' Kirsty's sobs were nearing hysteria.

Lewis looked to Sonia in despair. They had never known Kirsty to have any sort of tantrum. If anything, she was too quiet.

'But *why* can't you go to bed?' Sonia asked softly.

'Because she promised! She *promised* she'd come!'

'Who did?' Lewis asked.

'Mummy did! She said she'd come

180

back for my birthday, and bring me a nice present.' She continued to cry into Lewis's chest. He picked her up gently.

'Come on upstairs, poppet. Daddy will look after you.' He looked at Sonia with anguish in his eyes. Her heart contracted, seeing him suffer so. Then he took the sobbing child upstairs, murmuring comforting words to her.

Sonia picked up the toys and gifts the other children had brought and stacked them in a corner. Then she sat down, hugging her arms around her. It looked as if she'd been wrong about Juliette's total lack of motherly feeling. Sonia believed that she really had made that promise, and that Kirsty hadn't just made it up from wishful thinking.

It only served to confirm her grandmother's idea that Juliette hadn't taken her own life, yet it seemed to take Lewis completely by surprise that she had spoken to Kirsty and promised to return. Was he shocked because he really believed that Juliette had committed suicide, or was it because he hadn't realised that she had spoken to Kirsty before she left? If he was to blame for her death, it could make things very difficult if Kirsty started to tell more people that Juliette had meant to be here for her birthday.

It was almost an hour before he returned downstairs. Sonia put her book down as soon as he opened the door.

'Is she all right?'

'She's asleep at last.' Lewis sighed. 'But it was very hard. I tried to explain to her that Juliette was in heaven, and that people can't come back from heaven, no matter how much they love us. I tried to make her believe that her mother was watching over her, even though Kirsty couldn't see her. I hope it was the right thing to say.'

'Poor Kirsty — I never realised that she still thought Juliette would come back. Did she tell you what Juliette actually said when she left?'

Lewis turned to face her, frowning. 'Sonia, I don't want her upset any more. She must have been mistaken.'

'But, Lewis . . . '

'I forbid you to question her!' he snapped. 'She's had enough heartbreak. I don't want any more wounds opened. She's little more than a baby, and I just want her to recover from her grief.'

So saying, he stalked from the room. Sonia found she was shaking. Surely he didn't believe that she would have questioned Kirsty, knowing how upset the child was? But the thought crossed her mind — maybe he was trying to divert her from the idea that Juliette had meant to come back, and that her death had been caused by someone else. She rested her head on her hands. Yet again the evidence seemed to be pointing to Lewis, and it broke her heart to admit it.

He was polite enough to Sonia the next day, but she felt that he was distant. Those passionate kisses before he had gone on holiday felt so long ago, now. The evenings were beginning to draw in, and no matter how much Sonia kept her ears and eyes alert, no more clues about Juliette's death were forth-coming.

Laura appeared one evening, asking to see Lewis. They spent some time in his study, then came into the drawing room, where Sonia was sitting with her grandmother.

'Laura has a proposal to make to us, and I thought you would like to give your opinion before we can make a decision.'

'It's our opera production at the end of October. You know how important Juliette was to our company. We were wondering if you would mind if we dedicate our performances to her memory. We'd also like to put something about her in the programme — what do you think?'

There was a brief silence as the two women considered the offer. It was im-possible to see from Lewis's impassive expression what he himself thought.

'I think that would be a very gener-ous gesture,' Sonia ventured. 'What do you think, Granny?'

Felicity nodded. 'I agree. It's right that her talent should be remembered. But nothing should be said about how she died.'

'Don't worry, Mrs. Landale.' Laura leaned towards Felicity, gathering her hands with an impulsive gesture. 'It's her life we want to honour.'

'Well, I think that would be a fitting tribute. What about you, Lewis?'

'I'm happy for you to do that. But no speeches — only a mention of her in the programme.'

'Of course. You'll all be invited as guests. I'll bring you the tickets for whichever night you choose. It runs from Tuesday to Saturday.' She shrugged into her jacket, walking to the door. 'Oh, I'll be giving a party after the last performance, at our house. You're all invited.'

While Lewis showed her to the door, Felicity chuckled. 'That's typical of Laura. She loves organising things.' Then for a moment she looked wistful. 'I think she's taken over the pedestal vacated by

Juliette. They were perhaps a little too alike.'

'It seems a little odd — giving a performance in memory of someone who's died, and then inviting their relations to a party.'

Felicity smiled. 'I don't think you should worry about that, dear. Juliette would have loved the opportunity of a party. I hope you'll all go and enjoy yourselves, and remember her with happiness for once.'

12

In the lead-up to the opera performance, Lewis had gone to the Kendalls' house for a so-called 'working supper', and Laura had arrived unannounced once or twice at weekends when she knew that Lewis would be at home. They would disappear into his study to discuss the arrangements, and Sonia couldn't help wondering what else was going on behind the closed door.

Seeing them laughing together, Laura usually touching Lewis's arm in a gesture of affection, Sonia was angry with herself for minding. It wasn't as if she and Lewis were involved. It was perfectly acceptable for Laura to throw herself at him, wasn't it? If only she could really believe her own reasoning, and ignore the ache of resentment that never seemed to go away.

It was several weeks since she had

seen Tim, and she found her spirits lifting when he roared up to the door on his motorbike the week before the opera. She could do with his entertaining company.

'Hi, Tim, how are you?'

'Glad to get away from exhibitions for a couple of days. But I'm back on the road on Thursday. There's an international rugby match in London, and some guy wants me to do a painting of it.'

'That's great for you.' It was a surprise to her to find that she was feeling a little disappointed. It would have been nice to have him around for a while.

'You look a bit out of sorts, Sonia. Something bugging you?'

She flung herself on to the settee with a sigh. 'Oh, I'm just feeling a bit fed up at the moment. I'm finding the office work really tedious, and can't wait to get back to my ballet students.'

'Hey, yes. Michaela told me about that. Do you think I could come and sketch them some time?'

'Of course you can. Maybe you could bring some of your other sketches to show them.'

'I'll be back for the party. We can make a date then. In the meantime, I must see Michaela.' As he reached the doorway, he paused. 'We're going out for a meal later. How about coming with us?'

She grimaced. 'I'd have liked that, but Lewis is going to a meeting tonight and I said I'd babysit.'

He shrugged. 'Never mind. We'll get together properly when I get back from London — tomorrow's packed to the limit. See you!'

Sonia turned back to the window. The situation with Tim continued to perplex her. She had the feeling that he was still interested in her, though he hadn't openly made a pass at her recently. But he frequently went out with Michaela. It wasn't just an agent and client relationship, that was clear — there was definitely much more when they were together.

Kirsty was in bed in good time, tired after a busy day at school. Her grandmother was upstairs in her own room, listening to the radio in bed. Sonia sat in the drawing room, flicking through the television guide to see if there was anything she wanted to watch, when the strident ring of the telephone made her jump. There was an extension on the coffee table, so she lifted the receiver quickly, before it could disturb anyone upstairs.

'Hello?'

'May I speak to Lewis Gordon, please?'

'I'm sorry, he's out at present. May I take a message?'

The woman paused. 'I'm not sure . . . I really did want to speak to Lewis.' Sonia waited. 'Is that Michaela Landale?'

'No, it's Sonia Landale, Juliette's cousin.'

'Juliette's *cousin!*' The caller sounded startled. 'Are you the ballet dancer?'

'I don't dance any more. I'm living here now. Who are you?'

'Oh, I'm sorry, how rude of me. My name's Angela Singleton. I'm ... I mean, I *was* Juliette's close friend when my husband and I lived in Durham. We moved to London about two years ago, but Craig's business took him to Oman last year, and I decided to go with him. We just got back into the country at the end of September. A letter from Laura Kendall was waiting for us, inviting us to the show as it was a memorial to Juliette. I couldn't believe that she was ... dead.' Angela's voice cracked a little, and there was a pause while she gathered herself. Sonia's heart was thumping. A close friend of Juliette's! Maybe she would be able to discover something significant by talking to her.

'Were you thinking of coming to the show?'

'That's what I was ringing Lewis about. Craig and I are coming up for a few days, and we're going to make a point of being there on Saturday. We've really only stayed in the country long enough to see the children into boarding school, and our eldest girl, Claire, has just started university. But then we're off to the States for two months.'

'Shall I get Lewis to telephone you when he arrives home?'

'No, just tell him we'll be there — and that we're so dreadfully sorry to hear about Juliette.' Angela's voice trembled.

'Of course I'll pass on your message, Angela,' she said gently.

'Will you be there on Saturday?' Now she sounded anxious.

'Yes, of course I will.'

'I must see you . . . There's something . . . It's very important.'

Sonia agreed to see Angela on Saturday, and once they had said their farewells, put the phone down. Her pulse was racing. This was an unexpected development. But why did she want to talk especially to Sonia?

It seemed a long wait until Saturday, but finally Sonia found herself in the theatre, the lights darkened, for the production of *Carmen*. It was a good, surprisingly professional standard of performance. Juliette's name was mentioned in the programme, along with a photograph and a brief account of her contribution to the society. The tragedy of her cousin's death suddenly struck Sonia deeply. When she saw Laura on the stage, and imagined Juliette in her place, her eyes began to sting with tears. She wiped one eye surreptitiously, and noticed Lewis's head turn slightly. Then his hand patted hers gently, and came to rest on top with a firm hold. A huge lump rose in her throat at this gesture. Surely that wasn't the action of a murderer!

Sonia felt drained by the emotion of the occasion, and if she had not arranged to meet Angela Singleton at Laura's house, would have been quite happy to go home with her grandmother. Felicity obviously felt much the same, as she leaned heavily on Sonia's arm while they waited for Lewis to bring the car round. A few people had stopped to murmur their condolences to them, and to comment on Juliette's 'wonderful' voice. It was a relief when Lewis's car came into view and she could take her grandmother away from this further ordeal.

Once home, Lewis looked in on Kirsty, and made sure that Mrs. Howe was comfortable in the nursery sitting room. Sonia changed into a sleeveless black dress, fluffing out her hair, which had grown below her shoulders. It had reverted to its natural mid-blonde, the red rinse now faded completely. They joined Michaela in Lewis's car. As they drove round, Sonia's spirits were heavy as she wondered whether she would see tangible proof of the growing closeness between Lewis and Laura.

The sound of voices raised in laughter and conversation met them when they entered the house. Someone was playing Cole Porter on the piano, accompanied by the clink of glasses. Bill Kendall was wandering round with a wine bottle, topping up any glasses that caught his eye. He waved to the Landale group, but at that moment a woman caught his arm and pulled him away from them.

Lewis headed for the drawing room, with Michaela in his wake. Just as she was about to follow, Sonia felt a hand on her arm.

'Well, you do look great,' Tim's voice said in her ear. 'Promise me the first dance before anyone else claims it.'

She whirled round, her heart lifting. Tim looked almost out of place here, his dark hair curling over his shoulders, his tanned face split by a wide grin. He was wearing a light blue collarless silk shirt and navy blue linen trousers, which looked surprisingly exotic amongst the more sober dress of the other men.

'I don't know if it's a dancing sort of party,' she answered with a twinkle in her eye, 'but I promise if there is any, you'll be first on my list.'

'Well, let me get you a drink. Where are they serving them?'

'Perhaps in the kitchen. I saw . . . Oh!'

Tim stopped as Sonia froze in horror. 'What is it?'

Sonia was rooted to the spot, staring at Lewis, who was kissing Laura's cheek in greeting.

'Look . . . It's Laura. *She's wearing Juliette's bracelet.*'

Laura's hand was resting on Lewis's arm as he brushed her cheek with his lips. The sleeve of her dress had fallen back, revealing the distinctive gold filigree with the inlaid rubies and diamonds, sparkling against her golden skin.

Despite her anguish at seeing them so intimate, and the shock of the bracelet, Sonia became aware of Tim's fingers digging into her bare arm.

'My God, I don't believe it! How could she . . . ?' His voice was barely more than a whisper above the babble of voices.

The thoughts tumbled around Sonia's mind. Had Juliette passed it on to Laura? Or had Lewis given it to her? If he hadn't, then why was he so calm about her wearing it? How could they explain that Laura was wearing his dead wife's bracelet? Feeling sick, she turned to Tim.

'You must find out where she got it from. Will you please, Tim? I don't think I could ask.' She was trembling.

His face was grim. 'You bet I will. Wait here.' He strode over to their hostess, who was now standing alone, looking towards the door for new arrivals. Sonia saw them greet each other, Tim seeming very relaxed as he chatted for a few moments then pretended to notice the bracelet. She gave an animated explanation, extending her arm to examine the bracelet appreciatively. Finally, with a smile and a nod, he left her.

Sonia had retired to the conservatory doors, half hiding herself behind a tall palm. Tim grabbed two glasses from a tray which one of the waitresses was carrying past.

'She said she found it last month in a tiny antique jewellery shop in Hexham, when she was on one of her buying trips for a client.' He handed her one of the glasses. 'She'd always admired it, so she bought it. According to her, she told Lewis about it in case he didn't know it was in the shop, for sale. She'd wondered if he wanted it for Kirsty. But apparently he said no, to go ahead and wear it.'

'But how could she? Everyone would recognise it as being Juliette's.'

'Ah, but don't you see? Miss Kendall wants to step into your cousin's shoes, and I'm not just talking about her singing. Wearing her bracelet would give her the feeling of getting closer.'

Sonia shivered. It looked as if Lewis and Laura were very close already. If it hadn't been for meeting Angela, she would leave at once.

'Look, why don't I go and get us some supper? These things look better on a full stomach.'

She nodded, not because she was hungry, but because she felt the need to be alone for a few minutes. Laura's story was entirely plausible, but of course it could just be a fabrication. Yet if it were true, it meant that someone had sold the bracelet. Had it been Juliette? Or had it been her murderer? She could hardly believe that her cousin would part with the bracelet she always wore when singing, to bring luck.

'Hello — I believe you're Sonia Landale.'

Sonia whirled round, finding herself face to face with a woman in a long dark blue dress. It was elegantly plain, sleeveless, with a small gather over each shoulder. Her hair was skilfully streaked to give the impression of natural blonde, her make-up expertly applied. If this was Angela, she certainly didn't look old enough to have a daughter at university.

'Yes, I'm Sonia.'

The newcomer held out a hand with perfectly manicured nails. 'Angela Singleton. We didn't arrive until the end of the interval — Craig's business held us up. I saw you with Lewis.'

'Have you spoken to him yet?'

'Yes, I left Craig with him.' Looking

round furtively, she suddenly grasped Sonia's hand and pulled her further into the conservatory.

'When did you return to Alderburn?'

'May.'

'When you heard about Juliette?'

'No . . . no, I didn't know. I'd been trying to phone to tell them I was coming, but there was never any reply, so I just turned up. It was awful — it was the evening of the funeral. It was a terrible shock for me — and for them. No one knew I would be arriving.'

'How terrible for you. So you'd decided to make it up with her?'

'What do you mean?' Sonia asked sharply.

Angela sighed. 'She told me just about everything before I moved away. I knew she had treated you badly, and I told her so. But you know Juliette. Everything to do with singing came first. It didn't matter what else got in the way. That was just incidental.'

'But that's what she was always like. Richard was important to me — but she destroyed it all for a whim, and it didn't mean anything to her. That's what was so hurtful.' There were tears in Sonia's eyes as the memory of the betrayal returned to her. 'I don't know if I could have forgiven her completely. I came for Granny's sake, because our quarrel made her unhappy. I was prepared to try and see if we could be friends again, to see if she could have any remorse in her.'

Angela stretched out her hand to touch Sonia's shoulder. 'I'm afraid that I didn't believe her for a while, and that's why I didn't reply to her emails. Then they stopped coming, so I thought she was cross with me, too. Of course, that was when she . . . ' Angela took a deep breath to still her emotion. 'But on reflection, I do believe that she was always sorry, and it weighed heavily on her for a long time. Your accident was a great shock to her. She just didn't know how to find the right words to apologise. I know she would have been glad that you had decided to see her.'

'I . . . I never realised.' Granny had said that too — that Juliette had wanted to apologise. Maybe it had been true.

'Is this what you wanted to tell me?'

'Part of it. I thought you should know, if you didn't already. But I wanted to know what you thought about the time leading up to her death.'

'What do you mean?'

Angela worked her slim fingers anxiously together. 'I just can't believe that Juliette, of all people, could take her own life. Don't you feel that?' she appealed.

'It . . . certainly was . . . unlike her.' Sonia was cautious in her reply. She stroked the stem of her glass.

'It's just . . . She seemed to be so full of life, with so many things going for her. Her marriage — yes, it was in trouble. But there had been problems from the beginning, we know that, and it was inevitable that they would part at some time. She didn't keep in touch often, but after I received Laura's letter, I opened the last email Juliette sent, in

April. She was very happy.'

'Why was that?'

'You see, Juliette had a lover. I printed off a copy for you. Go on, read it.'

13

Sonia took the paper with trembling fingers. Juliette had mostly written about her singing. Then she wrote:

'I had thought that I was too busy for romantic attachments. But I've had a new man in my life for the past few months, and it's been wonderfully exciting. I'm not sure if he is important enough to come before my career. No matter what, I can't stay with Lewis. I have plans in hand for a new life, so don't be alarmed if you don't hear from me for a while. I'll email you once I have everything sorted out.'

The two women looked at each other.

'That wasn't written by a woman contemplating suicide,' Angela said.

'I know.' Sonia folded the paper again. 'May I keep this?'

'Yes, of course. If only she'd told me

more. If we knew the name of her lover, perhaps he could help us. I'm sorry to turn things upside down like this.'

'No, you haven't. I've been convinced for some time that she didn't commit suicide. But the alternative is horrible.' Sonia shivered as she slipped the paper inside her evening bag.

'Are you sure it wasn't an accident?'

'Definitely. Her things were replaced in her room secretly after I arrived — her suitcase appeared in the wardrobe, and her clothes in the drawers. Then Kirsty kept saying that Juliette had told her she would be back. The poor little thing was devastated when she didn't turn up on her birthday as promised.'

'Oh, God, that's terrible.' Angela pressed her knuckles to her lips. 'Who else knows?'

'Well, strangely enough it was my grandmother who first put forward the notion. She thought that Juliette was exceptionally happy in those last few weeks.'

'Planning a new life, not to end it.'

Sonia nodded. 'But I haven't told anyone else, much as I'd like to share the burden. Granny is too frail to be involved. The police have written off her death as suicide.'

'What does Lewis think?'

'Lewis . . . Well, if you look at the facts,' Sonia said, biting her lip, 'he has more motives than anyone. Juliette was leaving him — and she wanted to sell the house, against his wishes.'

Angela reached out one hand and grasped Sonia's tightly. 'I'm so sorry. It's a terrible thing. But I can hardly believe that Lewis . . . ' There were tears in her eyes. 'What are you going to do?'

Sonia felt instinctively that she could trust Angela. 'I'll just follow any lead I can. The latest is that Laura Kendall supposedly bought Juliette's good luck bracelet in a jewellery shop in Hexham.'

'So *that's* how she got it!'

Sonia saw Tim weaving through the crowd with two plates of food. 'My friend's returning.'

Angela squeezed Sonia's arm. 'I'm so glad we had the opportunity to talk. I hope you manage to unravel this mystery. I'll keep in touch.' She slipped away, murmuring a brief greeting to Tim as she passed.

Tim had brought two plates piled with food. Sonia picked at the contents of her plate for a few minutes, then pushed it aside. Tim, tucking into his ravenously, noticed that she wasn't eating.

'Don't you like what I brought you?'

She sighed. 'No, it's not that. I'm just not hungry. Neither am I in the mood for a party.'

'Come on, I'll take you home.'

'I don't want to spoil it for you.'

'Rubbish! Who do I know here? Just your family and Laura. You wait here while I get your coat.'

Sonia gave in. With a pang, she saw that Lewis was chatting with Laura and two other women. As she watched, their hostess laughed and put a proprietary hand on Lewis's arm. Sonia closed her eyes. If only she could put Lewis out of her mind.

They took the long way home, walking down the main road. The moon was full in a clear sky, and lit the route adequately. Sonia was content to walk in silence, listening to the rustling of the hedgerows in the breeze, and the ring of their footsteps on the road.

'Who was that you were talking to when I brought the food?' he eventually asked.

'That was Angela Singleton. She's a friend of Juliette's from a few years back.'

'So *that's* Angela.'

Sonia looked at him, surprised. 'You know about her?'

He shrugged. 'Oh, Michaela mentioned her. She thought it was odd that Angela hadn't been in touch since Juliette's death, especially with all the publicity surrounding it.'

'She and her husband were in the Middle East. They had fallen out, and she didn't read any emails. Angela didn't find out until Laura contacted her about the tribute.'

'So you know her, too?'

'No, she wanted to see me. She wanted to ask me about what happened.'

Tim gave her a quizzical look. 'It seems an odd thing to me, to want to talk to you. After all, you hadn't spoken to Juliette for over a year before she died.'

'Look, Tim, is this some sort of inquisition? She only wanted to ask how the family were.' Sonia couldn't help snapping at him. Her nerves were becoming frayed by his questioning, and she hated lying.

He gave her a strange look, as if puzzled by her outburst, then shrugged. 'OK, if you feel that way. I was just being interested.'

Tim was silent for the rest of their walk. When they reached the door of Alderburn Hall, he touched her shoulder gently.

'Shall I come in with you?'

'No, thanks. It was good of you to see me home, but I really am tired.'

His hand crept up to her hair. Sensing that he was preparing to kiss her, she stepped back quickly, pretending that she hadn't noticed. 'Goodnight, Tim.'

'Night.' His voice came thinly from the darkness, and his features blurred into the gloom. Sonia slipped inside the front door, closing it quietly behind her.

The next project was to find out more about the bracelet. Sonia searched on the internet for antique shops in the Hexham area, and found two that specifically dealt with jewellery. Later in the week, when she had a free afternoon, she looked out a photograph of Juliette, and printed off another one that she had taken of the others in the garden during the summer. Laura and Tim had both been there for Sunday lunch, and it also showed Michaela and Lewis.

The abbey town of Hexham was busy on this afternoon. Sonia looked round the shops and bought herself a pair of trousers and some new shoes, so that she had a legitimate reason for visiting the town. The first three antique shops she visited brought no joy in her search. There was another jewellery shop on the outskirts of the town, next door to an antique shop, so she stopped the car there on her homeward journey. This time, the owner's face lit with recognition when she produced the photo of Juliette.

'Yes, I remember that piece. A lovely item, early Edwardian. And this is the lady who brought it in.'

Delighted at this result, Sonia questioned him eagerly. 'Do you remember how she seemed? Was she disappointed to be parting with it?'

He frowned. 'No, I don't think so. She was very business-like. She had a pretty good idea of the value, and it took us a fair while to agree on the price. I paid her cash, as she wanted.'

Then he noticed the other photograph. 'I recognise this lady, too.' He pointed to Laura. 'She bought it from me a few weeks ago . . . and wait, I've seen this man.' His finger moved along to Lewis. 'He came in recently, asking the same sorts of questions as you did.' He looked up suspiciously. 'It's not stolen, is it?'

'No, nothing like that,' Sonia reassured him. 'We just can't understand why my cousin sold it. She loved that bracelet.'

'Well, sometimes circumstances mean we have to part with the things we treasure. I've had women in here selling their wedding rings when times are really tough.' He handed back the photographs. 'She got a good price. It would have paid for something very special.'

So Lewis had been asking questions as well. Obviously he'd wanted to verify Laura's story, too. Yet it was possible that he was trying to find out if Juliette had told anyone that she was going away. If it became clear that she hadn't committed suicide, then the enquiry into her death would be opened again.

It was lucky that he had come here before Sonia. If he discovered that she was investigating, then he would find out that she knew Juliette had been murdered. Would that make her a target? She shivered, remembering the ballet mirror incident. That could well have been a message to her that she was on dangerous ground.

Sonia spent the evening with her grandmother. The old lady was restless, saying that her bones ached. By about eleven o'clock she was more comfortable, after Sonia had helped her with a bath and had brought her a hot drink. She stayed with her until she dozed off, then turned down the lights and made her way back to the nursery wing.

She didn't bother putting on the light, knowing that most of the household would be in bed by now as it was almost midnight. As she passed the landing window she glanced down into the garden and froze as she saw a flicker of torchlight by the outbuildings. There was no moon and the night was overcast. All she could make out was that the figure was wearing trousers, and moved from the barn to the dilapidated sheds, then further round the house to the patio and main gardens.

The torch flicker disappeared as the prowler went out of her line of sight. Waiting for a few minutes, she wondered whether she ought to tell someone about their visitor. Realising that she had been standing at the window for some time, Sonia was just about to move when she saw the torch flicker again in the garden. Now it was moving back towards the house, to the kitchen door. A faint groan of hinges reached her ears, as the owner of the torch came inside. Then she became aware that the footsteps were crossing the hallway. Her heart beating faster, Sonia quickly slid behind the heavy curtains. The footsteps approached her and passed by.

A door opened. Peering from behind the curtain, Sonia saw a light spring on, illuminating a figure entering one of the bedrooms. It was Lewis. Then the door closed, and the corridor was once more in darkness. Sonia hurried past before he could emerge again. What could he have been doing at this time of night? Was this another incident to prove his guilt? Or was he just doing a routine check on the premises? Feeling confused, she tried to shut the conflicting thoughts from her mind.

Sonia felt the need to do some serious thinking. The next day, a prospective buyer was coming to look at the hall. It was a damp, cool autumn day with a hint of mist. Sonia decided to take a walk round the grounds before they arrived, to savour the atmosphere of the changing colours of the trees. As she was putting on her coat, she met Michaela coming in the front door.

'Going out?'

'I'm just having a breath of air. If you see Lewis, tell him I'll be in the rose garden.'

It was a dry day, but overcast. The

trees had turned to gold and bronze, the occasional russet hue warming the tones. Dry leaves of all colours crackled beneath her feet. Sonia sauntered round the hall, taking more notice of the building now that the time was approaching when she would have to leave it. For the first time she began to seriously consider what she could do with her future.

The typing job would come to an end in February. She ought to look for more work, but what was available to her? She only felt really alive when she was with her ballet students, but there was no more work available at the dance studio. The other two teachers were happy in their work and unlikely to leave, and there wasn't enough business to bring in a third full-time.

She could possibly scrape together enough to buy a small flat with her share of the capital from the sale of Alderburn Hall. Then again, Granny was her responsibility, and she would have to provide her with somewhere to live, as well as the care she needed as she aged. How could she possibly afford it?

Sonia paused on the terrace overlooking the rose garden. A few hardy bushes still displayed the odd bloom, but they would need pruning soon. They had been planted years ago when the Landales were doing well, and only needed routine maintenance now. They had always been Felicity's domain. If a developer bought the house, would he keep them, or would they disappear forever?

Then, with a pang, she thought of Kirsty. She'd grown to love the little girl as if she was her own. To see the light of happiness in the child's eyes when they met was magical. Turning back towards the house, she saw the little girl, running towards her with her coat flapping behind her. A smile of joy lit her rosy face, and her arms were lifted, ready for a hug.

Just as they were about to meet, Sonia became aware of a movement above her. Glancing upwards, to her horror, she saw one of the large stone spheres that decorated the roof of the house toppling towards her. With a cry she leaped forward, gathering Kirsty to her as she dived for safety.

The stone fell with a resounding crash, shattering on the terrace. Kirsty let out a high-pitched scream, clinging tightly to Sonia. Holding the sobbing child tightly, Sonia felt herself beginning to shake.

'Sonia! Are you all right? Is Kirsty hurt?' Michaela appeared beside them, her face anxious.

Gingerly Sonia sat up, still cradling the little girl. Murmuring comforting words, she stroked the dark red hair gently. 'We're fine, cherub. We're not hurt. It was just a silly accident.' Soon the words penetrated to Kirsty, who lifted a tear-stained face to Sonia.

'I want Daddy. Where is he?'

Sonia looked round anxiously. Where was Lewis? And who had pushed the stone from the roof?

14

'Come on, we'd better get you inside. Oh, look at your hands!' Michaela exclaimed.

It was then that Sonia realised how her knuckles were stinging. They had been skinned and the backs of her hands scraped when she fell forward with Kirsty. She stood up shakily.

Then she became aware of Lewis, running from the kitchen doorway. With a sob, Kirsty tore herself from Sonia's arms and launched herself at him. Scooping her up, he kept repeating, 'Are you hurt? Are you all right, sweetheart?'

'She's just frightened.' Michaela was curt. 'Sonia took the brunt of the fall — but escaped the falling stone.'

Lewis became very still, as his eyes took in the shattered masonry littering the path. 'Good God, what happened?'

'One of the stone orbs fell from the roof,' Sonia said quietly. 'Luckily I saw it and got out of the way.'

'This wretched house! The sooner we get rid of it, the better.' Then his expression registered concern. 'Thanks so much for saving Kirsty. You've no idea what it means . . . Oh, Sonia, your hands must be sore. We'd better get them cleaned right away.'

'I'll do it,' Michaela said, taking Sonia's arm. 'Your prospective buyer will be here any minute now. Leave the little one with us; she'll be fine.'

Lewis relinquished his daughter, who seemed content enough to go with Sonia now that she'd had reassurance from him. Hearing the sound of car tyres on the gravel, he disappeared round to the front of the house.

Sonia constantly relived the horrific incident throughout the rest of the day. It was doubtful that the stone could have fallen on its own. She found herself wondering if Lewis could possibly have been the one to push it.

He would have had time to get down the stairs from the roof, which was easily accessible from the attics.

Maybe it had been meant to frighten her away — or had it really been aimed to injure her? After all, she was the only one standing in the way of Kirsty's inheritance. He certainly had been shocked when he saw his daughter crying. Maybe he hadn't realised that she would run so quickly to the garden.

It was a great relief when Sonia's mother, Teresa, telephoned during the afternoon. 'Mum! How are you? Is the snow bad?'

'Not yet. I don't think I'll ever get used to it. That's one reason why I'm phoning. Dan and I were thinking of coming to England for Christmas. How would that fit in with your plans?'

'Oh, Mum.' Sonia swallowed the tears that threatened to overcome her. 'I'd love it. Do you want to stay here at the hall?' How wonderful to have their calm, loving presence at this time, especially after the morning's incident.

'It's a nice thought, but I know some of the rooms are closed up. No, we'll find a hotel nearby, hire a car and do a bit of driving around on our own. We'll feel freer that way.'

'But you must spend Christmas with us. It won't be any trouble at all. After all, it is partly my house — and this will probably be the last time we spend Christmas here.'

'I'd love to be in the old place again. But how about you coming away with us for a few days over New Year? You haven't really had a holiday this year, and it would be a break for you.'

'That would be great. Would you like me to book somewhere for you? We'll have to hurry, as hotels are very busy at that time of year.'

'Thanks, dear. Even a cottage would do. I don't need luxury.'

Sonia's mood had lifted by the time she replaced the receiver. At least she would be able to relax with her mother and stepfather, without the constant worry of searching for clues and trying to support others.

Lewis looked pleased when she told him about their prospective visit. He suggested that she should ask Laura Kendall about local hotels, as she often had dealings with them in her interior design business.

Sonia rang her during the week, and was invited over to the farmhouse for a meal. It was with mixed feelings that she made her way there. She hadn't been back since the party, when Lewis and Laura had looked so intimate, and she had seen the bracelet on Laura's wrist.

Laura welcomed Sonia effusively, ushering her into the conservatory for a drink before supper.

'My father's out tonight, so it's just you, me and Mummy. How lovely that your mother's coming over for Christmas. It must be ages since you saw her.'

'Yes, it's about eight months. But we keep in touch by telephone and email.'

'You must bring her, and your stepfather, here when they arrive. My parents would love to meet them.'

'Of course,' Sonia murmured, surprised at this invitation. She had always thought that Laura saw her as a rival for Lewis's affections, so it seemed incongruous to offer hospitality to her mother.

Mrs. Kendall left them alone once the meal was over. Laura showed her the brochure for a small hotel that she had recently decorated. It had been taken over by new owners a few months earlier, and she thought it would be modest, but comfortable for the Canadian visitors. 'If you mention my name, they'll fall over themselves to help you.'

Sonia thanked her, finding Laura's manner to be less bossy than in the past. At that moment, Mrs. Kendall appeared in the doorway. 'Sorry to disturb you girls, but that's Leo on the phone. Do you want to speak to him now, darling?'

Sonia was amazed at the transformation of Laura's expression. Her eyes sparkled, her cheeks went pink, and her mouth opened in a delighted smile. 'Leo! Oh, you'd better tell him that I'll call him back later.'

Laura's mother went to relay the message. Sonia reached for her handbag. 'It's getting late — time I went home. Thanks for the advice about the hotel — and the meal was lovely.'

'Oh, you mustn't hurry away, Sonia. Leo won't mind at all if I ring him later.' Her voice became silky at the mention of his name.

Sonia smiled. 'I can see that he's important. Don't keep him waiting too long.'

Laura laughed, blushing. 'You've found me out. Oh, Sonia, I think he's going to be someone very special.'

'So how long have you known him?'

'Only a few weeks. You won't believe this, but he's Daddy's dentist! About a month ago we met at a dinner party, and he took me to the theatre a week later. Since then we've seen each other most days. He's just adorable!'

Sonia felt as if a great weight had

lifted from her. So there had been nothing in the friendship between Laura and Lewis! Just to make sure, she mentioned Laura's new boyfriend to him the next day, and he looked delighted.

'It's time Laura had someone to run around after! She'll make a wonderful wife, with all her organisational skills.'

'Is that what you think makes a good wife?' Sonia teased, laughing.

'Well, in Laura's circles, it certainly does. It'll be interesting to see how things progress.'

He gave a small chuckle, walking off towards his study. As usual, her heart gave a little flip. If only her investigation could be resolved, she would feel able to give rein to her feelings for Lewis at last.

Christmas was approaching fast, and she had to start thinking about preparations. Kirsty was becoming involved in activities at school, and with the Sunday School. Also, she was taking part in a display with the ballet school. Sonia was treated like one of the mothers, being so involved with costumes and taking her to classes. It was a disturbing feeling — something she could enjoy, but she was afraid to let herself relax into the role. After all, things would be changing dramatically once they had sold the house.

The ballet display took place on the first Saturday in December. Lewis and Sonia sat together for the concert, smiling proudly at each other when Kirsty performed her part gracefully and neatly.

'You were right — she does have a natural ability,' he said as they applauded. 'It must run in the family.'

'I'm glad you enjoyed it. She certainly is a natural, and it's given her a lot of confidence.' Here they were, talking as if they were both her parents! Sonia shook herself mentally. *Don't even think of it.*

'I can see that. A year ago, I wouldn't have believed that she could do this.'

The applause died away as the next class took their places. Last on the programme was Sonia's advanced group. Sitting, biting her lips throughout the performance, she willed them to dance every step as they had rehearsed. As the last dancer sank to the floor in the final pose, she gave a sigh of relief. They had been magnificent! The applause came in great waves, and she became aware of Lynn and Verity, her colleagues, waving to her to come to the front of the hall.

As she acknowledged the extra surge of applause, Sonia felt a pang of nostalgia. It was a bittersweet reminder of her days on the stage. But today it didn't matter that she hadn't performed herself. These youngsters were her own creation, smiling and applauding her from the stage. She brought them forward for another bow, then let them take their well-deserved acclaim for themselves.

Once the grateful dancers and their parents had let her go at the end of the concert, she returned to the foyer where Lewis and Kirsty were waiting. Lewis's face was full of pride, but to her astonishment he wasn't looking at Kirsty — he was smiling at Sonia as she came towards him.

'Congratulations. Your dancers were superb.'

'They were wonderful, weren't they?'

'Yes, but you made them so. I heard everyone talking about it. They said that the senior class had never looked so polished and professional.'

Her cheeks warmed. 'Did they really?' Looking into his face, she felt that this man could surely not have tried to harm her — could he?

Once they were back at the house, Lewis showed her a leaflet. 'I was wondering . . . the Northumbrian Ballet is doing a season in Newcastle, and I thought you might be interested in going. It's on next week.'

Panic fluttered through her. She hadn't been to a professional ballet performance since her own days as a dancer. Would it be unbearably distressing to watch from the other side of the footlights?

Lewis noticed her hesitation. 'It doesn't matter, if you'd rather not. But

I thought maybe, now you're a teacher and choreographer, that you would feel able to enjoy it.'

Pushing away her doubts, she smiled. 'You're right. It's time I started behaving like a successful teacher, instead of a failed performer. Which night shall we go?'

He looked relieved and happy at her reply. As they made their plans, Sonia had a sudden thought.

I'm actually going on a date with Lewis.

The trip to the ballet was scheduled for two nights before the Canadian visitors arrived. Sonia wasn't sure whether she was feeling taut with excitement or apprehension as she prepared for their night out. It was difficult keeping her hand still as she applied her lipstick. Her feelings were a mixture of nervousness over being with Lewis, and of worrying about her own reactions upon seeing a professional company performing after all this time.

She examined her reflection carefully.

She had put on a little weight since stopping training seriously, but it suited her. Lifting her chin, she gazed at the mirror with pride. She'd fought back from injury, and now there was hardly a trace of a limp in her walk.

Kirsty rushed out of the drawing room to meet her as she descended the stairs. 'You look lovely, Auntie Sonia! Just like a fairy!'

Sonia laughed and hugged her. She supposed that her pale pink dress with its sequinned bodice looked quite fairy-like.

Lewis joined them at that moment, pulling on his coat. His eyes reflected his own appreciation of her outfit. 'I'm honoured to be accompanied by such a pretty lady,' he said especially for Kirsty's benefit. They both kissed her, then left her in Nicola's care for the evening.

As they passed the end of the drive-way, Lewis suddenly said, 'That reminds me. I forgot to tell you — Harry Neill came to see me today. He's moving out tomorrow. He and his wife are getting back together again, and they're going to live in Newcastle. He thinks he can get work with a builder he knows there.'

'Does Nicola know? She was very friendly with their daughter.'

'I haven't told her yet. Remind me to do that when we get back tonight.'

So Harry Neill was going! Now she had little chance of discovering if he was to blame for Juliette's death. Maybe that was why he was leaving — but no, he'd always been keen to see his wife again.

She pushed thoughts of the Neills from her mind as they enjoyed a Chinese meal before the ballet. Tonight she just wanted to forget about any suspicions of who could be responsible for Juliette's death.

Entering the theatre, she appreciated the sight of the plush interior, the ornate boxes, the golden lighting. Lewis was content to let her absorb the atmosphere without interrupting her thoughts, except for the occasional comment.

The lights dimmed at last, and the

orchestra began the introduction to the first ballet. It was one she had danced in herself, and her legs felt ready to form the steps as she watched the dancers. When the lights came up again, she found that Lewis was looking at her intently.

'What is it? Why are you looking at me like that?'

'Sorry . . . I was just wondering how you were feeling.'

She frowned. 'It's difficult to put into words. One part of me is longing to be on the stage, but the other half is content to observe and enjoy the beauty of the movement seen as a whole. I never really had the chance to do that when I was performing myself.'

'I wish I could have seen you dance.'

She smiled. 'Have you seen the *Sleeping Beauty* DVD?'

'Yes, once, many years ago. I'm sure I would appreciate it a lot more, now that I know you so much better.'

Stupidly, her heart began to beat faster at his words, and the intensity of his gaze. She looked down at her programme, saying, 'I wonder how long this interval is.'

'Only a few minutes, I think.' Lewis began to flick through his own programme, as if sensing that she was embarrassed by what he had said. At that moment, the lights dimmed again.

After the next ballet came the main interval. They opted to go to the bar for a drink as the theatre was hot. Lewis told her that he would queue while she stood near the door.

'I don't believe it — can it really be? Sonia Landale!'

Sonia swung round to see a tall, slim man, with greying hair, holding out one hand to her.

'David Rayner! I saw your name in the programme! So how are you enjoying being artistic director of the Northumbrian Ballet? It seems only yesterday that you were bossing us all around in London!'

'The past two years have flown!' he said as they touched cheeks. 'So how are you, my dear? I heard about your terrible accident.' His forehead was furrowed with concern.

'Well enough, David. But I won't dance professionally again.'

'I'm sorry to hear that. You had something special, you know. The Northumbrian Ballet would have given anything to have you with them.'

'They look as if they're doing fine without me,' she replied, smiling. It surprised her that his praise of her former ability didn't affect her as deeply as it might once have.

'So what are you doing with yourself now?'

'I've been doing some temporary office work, and recently took on some advanced coaching at a ballet school.'

'Really? Are you enjoying it?'

'Oh, yes, very much. If only I had more. The office work isn't really my scene.' She gave a small grimace.

'You know, the Northumbrian Ballet is doing one of Richard Hayling's ballets in February. It's *The Three Graces*.

You danced in the premier, didn't you?'

The mention of this work brought back bittersweet memories. Richard had created one of the roles especially for her.

'I did. It's a delightful work.' A wave of nostalgia swept over her as she remembered how much she had enjoyed dancing her part.

David looked thoughtful for a moment. 'I wonder if you would like to be artistic adviser for the ballet. We really could do with someone like you to give us some insight into the choreographer's ideas.'

'Isn't Richard going to help you?'

'No, he's going to the States in January to prepare a big new ballet in New York. It's quite a coup.'

'It certainly is!' Despite the way they had parted, she couldn't help feeling pleased for him. They had been close for so long. After only a moment's hesitation, she added, 'I'll be happy to help you.' It would be wonderful to enter the world of professional ballet again.

'Good! Telephone me after New Year,

and we'll sort out the details. I must go — loads of people to see.' Patting her arm, he dived off into the crowd.

'Who was that?' Lewis approached with their drinks.

Sonia was still feeling rather dazed. 'That was David Rayner. He's the artistic director of the Northumbrian Ballet. He's just offered me a job!'

'What?' The glasses trembled in Lewis's grasp.

'Oh, not dancing — as an artistic adviser. It may be for just one ballet, one that I danced in, in London. But it could be a real breakthrough.' Her eyes were shining as she took the first sip of her drink.

'That's brilliant. It's what you wanted, isn't it? A solicitor's office isn't really for you, is it?'

She regarded him in dismay. 'It's not that obvious, is it?'

He laughed. 'Don't worry, your work's fine, but I see you looking out of the window with a sort of longing, from time to time. And your happiness at the ballet display — you never look like that in the office.'

'You're right. I'll be quite glad when my time's up.' It was touching that he had read her so intimately.

He took her empty glass and placed it on a ledge with his own. 'That's just as it should be. You belong in an artistic world.'

She found herself laughing frequently on the way home. She felt as if she was sparkling from every surface of her body.

'This new job means a lot to you, doesn't it?' Lewis said as he unlocked the front door.

'After all this time, I can actually see a new beginning. You know, I think I may actually enjoy this even more than performing.'

'You're not serious!'

'Yes, really. I was always terribly nervous about dancing in public, you know. I never really admitted it to myself. It wasn't so bad in the corps de ballet, but once I became a soloist . . . '

'Well I never,' he said gently, stroking a strand of hair back from her forehead. 'I always thought you looked so poised and confident.'

'I learned to cope with it.'

Lewis suddenly bent his head towards her, and pulled her into his arms. With a sigh, she relaxed against his body. Then she seemed to hear her grandmother's words. *You haven't found any proof that he didn't kill Juliette.*

With a cry, she pushed him away. 'Lewis . . . I can't . . . not now.' Pushing open the front door, she ran into the house, leaving him standing, bewildered, on the doorstep.

15

Felicity was eager to hear all about the evening at the ballet, and was delighted at the news of Sonia's new job. Then she asked Sonia to bring down a box of letters from one of the attic rooms.

'What's in here, Granny?' Sonia placed the box on the table beside her grandmother.

Felicity's eyes lit up. 'Oh, a lot of old letters that mean something to me, but not to anyone else. Some of them are your grandfather Michael's. I thought that I ought to go through them again, and then maybe they could be burned. I don't want you young people to have such a tedious job when I'm gone.'

'Granny . . . '

'There's no point in being unrealistic.' Felicity waved away her protests. 'No-one can live forever, and I've had a pretty good run. It's been a great joy to me to have two such talented grand-daughters.' She held out her hand to Sonia, who took it and knelt beside her.

'I hope you won't leave us for a long time,' she said softly, her eyes bright.

'Well, then, it's time I knuckled down to work. Would you mind bringing over that small table by the window?'

As Sonia picked up the table, her eyes caught a movement in the yard below. Kirsty was walking across the path towards the barn where they kept the cars. As she reached the door, she opened it and slipped inside.

Sonia drew in her breath. What was the child up to? She knew full well that she wasn't supposed to go in there alone.

Quickly she brought the table over to her grandmother. 'I must dash, Granny — but I'll be back very soon.'

Felicity smiled dreamily, already in the process of reading one of the letters. Sonia saw no one else as she hurried down the stairs and outside. Who was supposed to be with Kirsty?

She reached the garage door to discover the little girl setting up the ladder to the loft.

'Kirsty! You know you're not allowed to go up there!'

'Please, Auntie Sonia. Mitten is stuck in the hayloft and I have to get her.'

'Your daddy would be cross if he knew you were climbing up there. Where is he?'

'He's gone over to the cottage to see if Mr. Neill has gone yet. I was watching a video with Aunt Michaela, but she told me to go and feed Mitten.'

'You should have fetched an adult as soon as you realised that she was in the loft. I'll go up.'

Taking the ladder from the child, she was just about to put her foot on the first rung, when she stopped. The rung in front of her eyes had been almost sawn through, and was held in place by the smallest possible strip of wood. It would never have taken Kirsty's weight. She caught her breath.

'What is it?' Kirsty asked.

'Nothing.' Sonia didn't want to frighten her. She began to climb, but stepped over the damaged rung. Sonia reached for the mewing cat as soon as she was within distance, and held the animal against her shoulder with one arm as she descended. Managing to avoid the damaged rung again, she handed the cat down.

'You naughty pussy!' Kirsty scolded as she hugged her pet close. 'You know you're not supposed to go up there! Daddy will be very cross with you!'

Sonia couldn't help smiling at the child's words. 'Off you go. I'm sure she'll be really hungry now.'

Once she was alone, Sonia removed the ladder from the hayloft, and tied it with a tight knot to a metal pipe. There was no way that Kirsty could move the ladder herself now. She was certain that this had been a carefully planned incident to injure Kirsty. But who would do such a thing — and why?

Then she remembered that she had seen Lewis out in the dark round the barn. He would have had ample opportunity to sabotage the ladder. Then she shook herself. How stupid she was! He would never willingly hurt his daughter. With a jolt, Sonia realised that at last she had proof that Lewis couldn't be to blame for the series of attempted accidents.

Surely that meant that he wasn't to blame for Juliette's death, either. She was certain that these sinister events were somehow linked. All at once, she felt like dancing for joy, as there was no need for her to hold back her feelings for him. The sinister cloud that had enveloped her evaporated in an instant. But there was no time for euphoria. It was urgent that she warn Lewis that someone seemed to be trying to cause harm to both Kirsty and herself.

Lewis was striding up the path from the cottage when she found him. His face lit with welcome, but became grim when she told him what had happened. Yet when they went down to the garage to examine the ladder, they found that the rung had been removed completely. 'This is really worrying. I always believed that my daughter would be safe at home.'

'We'll need to make sure that she's either with you or me.'

Lewis looked at her intently. 'You mean that you don't trust anyone else? What about Michaela?'

'I — I'm not sure. But even if we can trust her, she can't really be bothered with a six-year-old. Look what happened today.'

He nodded. 'I hardly ever leave her with Michaela for that reason. I only meant to be gone about twenty minutes, but by the time I checked all the rooms, it was nearly an hour.'

'What about Nicola? She has a connection with Harry Neill.'

'I trust Nicola implicitly. We've known her for years, and as far as I know she didn't like Neill. She was only friendly with his daughter. I suppose it could have been a parting gripe from him — but I haven't seen him round here for ages. Without anyone witnessing the sabotage, we've nothing to go on.'

'What are we going to do, Lewis?'

He sighed. 'I don't know, yet. I think we'd better just keep a watchful eye. It'll be easier with your parents here, I'm sure. I know you'll want to go places with them, but you can invite them for meals as often as you like. Let them feel really at home.'

'Thanks. I'm sure they'd like that.'

He caught her arm just before they entered the kitchen. 'I would have said that anyway, you know. It's not just for our protection.'

She smiled. 'I know. But it's nice to know they'll be welcome.' Letting her hand slide affectionately over his forearm, their eyes locked for a few moments before she turned away to push the door open. Much as she wished to, she couldn't afford to open up to Lewis yet. Her parents' arrival was imminent, and she still had one or two mundane tasks to complete before that.

Sonia collected Dan and Teresa from Newcastle Airport later that evening. As they were jet-lagged from the journey, she took them straight to their hotel. Sonia felt much happier as she left them for the fifteen-minute drive back to Alderburn. Just having them here made her feel more optimistic.

Kirsty had finished school for Christmas, with only a few days to go until the day itself. She had been shy at the appearance of two new people, but had soon taken to them both. Within a few days, the child was running to hug them whenever they appeared.

Michaela had known Teresa in the years after her husband's death, when she had lived at Alderburn, until she had met Dan and moved to Canada. Michaela, Dan and Teresa had an evening out together, which Teresa later told Sonia she had enjoyed very much.

'Is Michaela as you remember her, Mum? I'm not sure if I just see her differently because I'm an adult now.'

Teresa laughed. 'She's always had

style. But now you come to mention it, she does seem calmer than she used to be. She always struck me as being a bit reckless when she was younger.'

'In what way?'

'Oh, you know, wild parties, fast cars, a different man in tow every week.'

'I suppose you could be right. But she still drives a fast car!'

They watched Kirsty carefully on Christmas Day, worried that she might think that Juliette would be coming for Christmas. But when they mentioned Juliette, Kirsty seemed to have accepted that her mother was gone for good. They made sure that there were plenty of games, activities, and laughter. Felicity came downstairs for the Christmas meal, but retired early in the evening. Michaela had invited Tim, as he had nowhere else to spend the festival. Sonia noticed her mother watching the newcomer curiously, and soon saw them in conversation in a corner. Later she asked her mother what they had been talking about.

'Oh, I was wondering if he missed his family at this time of year. But it seems he's adopted, and he says he doesn't feel very close to his Australian family now. He'd rung them earlier today.'

'Yes, he told me that he was adopted. But he never said much about his parents. You must have a knack of drawing information out of people.'

Teresa gave a chuckle. 'It's the motherly method of gaining a young man's confidence. You're just too young!'

Sonia gave her a hug. It was so wonderful to have them with her.

They left for their New Year trip on the 30th December. Luckily the mild weather held, and the journey was easy. Their hotel in Derbyshire was small, and had no special celebrations put on for the turning of the year. This suited them fine, as they just wanted to have the freedom to do as they wished, and have a quiet time together.

On the morning of the first of January, Sonia telephoned Alderburn Hall to wish the occupants a happy New

Year. Lewis answered, and asked if they were enjoying their holiday.

'It's lovely here — so open and wild! Mum and Dan have gone walking this morning.'

'But not you?'

'No, the terrain is too rough for my leg. Did you celebrate last night?'

'No, once Kirsty was in bed I watched television for a while, but I didn't even stay up till midnight. Your grandmother was too tired to see in the New Year, and Michaela was out with friends. I would have felt a bit stupid toasting the New Year on my own.'

At his words, Sonia felt a great longing to be with him. She would have loved to celebrate with him. 'Is Granny there? I'd like to speak to her, as well.'

Lewis took the cordless phone up to Felicity so that they could chat for a few minutes. Feeling satisfied that all was well, Sonia relaxed for the rest of the day. As they ate their evening meal, Sonia began to talk about Tim with her mother.

'I just can't make out what it is between Michaela and Tim. I suppose he's her protégé, but sometimes I catch something more than that between them. I suspected at first that they were . . . well, possibly lovers, but she never seemed to mind if he took me out, and seemed to actively encourage it.'

'Maybe she feels protective towards him because he's such a long way from home,' Dan offered.

'No, I think it's more than that,' Teresa said, putting down her knife and fork. 'There was something I noticed — a definite likeness. You may think I'm crazy, but I think Tim is Michaela's son.'

There was a stunned silence. Then Sonia exclaimed, 'But that's impossible!'

'Is it?' Teresa responded. 'How old is he — late twenties? Michaela would have been in her late teens when he was born. He was adopted at birth — in this country — and was taken to Australia while he was still a baby.'

'And he could have traced his mother to Alderburn,' Dan added.

Sonia shook her head incredulously. 'I wondered about many things, but I never considered that.' Then she looked up suddenly. 'But Granny must have known! Michaela would have been living with Granny and Grandpa then.'

'Well, I expect they hushed it all up. After all, it wasn't something you broadcast in those days. She probably thought it gave Michaela a second chance if it wasn't known.'

'But how come no one knew within the family?'

'Michaela did go away to London for about a year, to train as a secretary. It's possible that she had the baby first, then did a crash course.'

At that moment, the waiter approached the table.

'I'm sorry to interrupt you, Miss Landale, but there's a telephone call for you. Do you want to take it in your room?'

Sonia pushed back her seat, jumping

to her feet. 'Yes, please.' An unexpected call could only mean one thing — bad news. Her stomach clenched with apprehension, she hurried along the corridor to her room. Grabbing the telephone, she quickly said, 'Hello?'

'Sonia? Sonia, are you there?' It was Felicity's agitated voice.

'Granny! What's the matter? Are you all right?'

'Oh, my dear, it was in the letters. I didn't know she'd written to him. He never told me — but it explains so much. But it's not true, you know, he wasn't her father . . . Oh!'

'Granny, who do you mean?' There was some sort of click on the line.

'I . . . can't speak now. But you'll see it for yourself. I've got to go.' The receiver clattered into place.

'Granny? Granny!' But it was too late. Only the disconnect tone sounded in her ear. Replacing the telephone, she sat on the bed, her mind whirling. What on earth had Felicity been trying to tell her? She reached out her hand to ring

Lewis immediately, then stopped. Perhaps it would be best to talk to Teresa and Dan first.

They congregated in the Draytons' room. Sonia related the call, then added, 'I think I heard some clicks, as if someone was listening in on an extension. I believe that's what frightened her.'

'But why on earth should she be frightened?' Dan asked, his forehead creased with a frown.

Sonia looked from one to the other. She would have to tell them everything — but she knew now that this was the right thing to do. Taking a deep breath, she related all that had happened since she returned to Alderburn.

'Why on earth didn't you tell us sooner?' Teresa exclaimed, reaching to touch her daughter's arm.

'It . . . seemed so far-fetched at first. But then as my own suspicions grew, I felt that there was no-one I could trust. And then of course, Lewis was my main suspect, and I didn't want to tell anyone. I just couldn't believe it was him.'

'Of course not!' Teresa exclaimed. 'He's the last person who I would believe could do away with his wife.'

'And you really wanted to clear his name, didn't you?' Dan said gently.

Sonia blushed. 'Yes, I did.'

Dan patted her hand. 'You may think you've been hiding your feelings, but your mother and I both realised that there's some kind of a spark between you two.'

'We didn't want to say anything until you mentioned it,' Teresa added.

'It hasn't come to anything. I know he finds me attractive, but we've had some difficult encounters, and I couldn't be positive he wasn't guilty until last week.'

'I think you should tell Lewis all this as soon as possible. I believe that the culprit is close to home, and that you and Kirsty are in danger,' Dan advised.

'You can't mean . . . Michaela?'

Teresa nodded. 'You need to find out why she kept her relationship with Tim a secret. I think you need to investigate that, and also to find out where Juliette was going when she left Alderburn.'

'What about this alleged lover?'

'Don't you think that could be Tim?' Teresa suggested, one eyebrow raised.

Sonia gasped. 'Of course! He mentioned her not long after we met, and I had the impression that he had admired her.'

Dan was looking concerned. 'I wonder if we should cut short our break.'

'Do you think Granny's in danger?'

He shook his head. 'No, but it would be a good idea to talk to Lewis as soon as possible.'

They agreed to telephone Alderburn the next morning.

But as Sonia was leaving the breakfast room, she was called to the telephone. It was Lewis. 'I'm sorry to bring you bad news, Sonia, but I'm afraid that your grandmother was taken into hospital this morning.'

'Oh, no! Is it serious?'

'I'm afraid so — it was a stroke. Michaela took in her breakfast, and found her unconscious. The doctor thinks it may have happened several hours ago.'

'Oh, Lewis.' Sonia's eyes filled with tears. 'We were planning on coming home today, anyway. Granny telephoned last night, and she sounded agitated.'

'What was that about?'

'Something about a letter. It was a bit garbled. Had she said anything to you?'

'Nothing at all.' He sounded puzzled. 'We'll talk about it when you arrive.'

'Lewis — do you mind if Mum and Dan stay at the hall?'

'No problem. I'll get a room ready. Drive carefully — we don't want anything happening to you.' His voice was gentle, making her want to weep at his concern for her. But she hadn't time for tears now.

It didn't take them long to pack and leave the hotel, but the journey back to County Durham seemed endless. The roads were busy with revellers travelling home after the New Year break, and with people returning to work.

Lewis must have heard the sound of the car wheels, because he was waiting on the front doorstep for them.

Sonia hurried towards him. 'How is she?'

His face was grave. 'I'm sorry. Michaela phoned from the hospital half an hour ago. She's gone.'

Sonia put one trembling hand to her mouth, then stumbled into Lewis's waiting arms. 'If only we'd come home last night, when she phoned.'

'It wouldn't have made any difference,' he said gently, holding her close.

'But she was upset when she called. I could have been with her, maybe sorted out what was troubling her.'

'I don't think anything would have helped. She was getting very frail, you have to admit that. Come on, we'll go inside.'

Teresa and Dan followed them into the house. 'Where's Kirsty?' Teresa asked as she wiped her eyes.

'She's playing with a school friend in Alderburn. I was going to take Sonia over to the hospital as soon as you arrived, and I didn't want her to be too upset by all the comings and goings.'

Teresa nodded. 'I think it would do us all good to have something to eat. I'll go into the kitchen and rustle something up. Have you had anything, Lewis?'

He shook his head. 'I was waiting for you.'

Dan offered to bring in the cases from the car, leaving Sonia and Lewis alone. They sat on the settee, her head on his shoulder.

'Don't feel bad about not being here when it happened,' he told her. 'The most important thing is that you returned to live at Alderburn when you did. It meant a lot to her, having you here. She would have gone much sooner if you hadn't returned.'

'Do you really think so?'

'I could see that you brought great happiness to her in these last few months. It helped make up for the shock of Juliette's death.'

She sat up suddenly. 'Lewis, there's something I have to tell you . . . '

'Not now,' he said gently. 'We'll have plenty of time to talk later. I think some hot food is the best thing for us, now.'

Michaela returned as they were clearing after a sombre lunch. Her face looked pale, devoid of make-up for once, which gave her a vulnerable appearance. Her eyes met Sonia's across the hallway.

'I'm sorry I wasn't here,' Sonia said.

Michaela shook her head. 'It wouldn't have made any difference. She never regained consciousness.'

Then the tears brimmed over in Sonia's eyes again. Seeing that, Michaela stepped towards her, and the two embraced for the first time since she had returned to Alderburn. Michaela gave a sigh, touching the younger woman's shoulder briefly, then moved away. She had never been very demonstrative, but Sonia felt it would have mended much if they could have shared their grief. Now any affection between them seemed to have slipped away for good.

After she had gone upstairs, and Teresa and Dan were unpacking in Juliette's room, Sonia asked Lewis to come for a walk with her. Once they were away from the hall, she began to speak. 'Lewis, there's so much I have to tell you. It's mainly because of Granny.'

She went on to tell him how her grandmother had confided in her about her suspicions concerning Juliette's death. As she began to unfold the story of how she came to believe Felicity's words, Lewis stopped walking, and interrupted her.

'But this is what I thought, too. Why on earth didn't you tell me? We could have pooled our ideas and our findings.'

'Oh, Lewis, I'm so relieved that you suspected it, too. But surely you realise why I couldn't have told you before?'

'You don't mean . . . You suspected *me?*' A look of outrage crossed his face. 'How could you!'

She turned away, hands thrust into her pockets. 'But you had the best motive, Granny kept saying, and I had to respect her opinion. I didn't want to think the worst of you, you've got to believe me! And I know Granny didn't want to either. Then . . . you were often so cold and unfriendly to me, I thought that you must have something to hide.'

He looked dismayed by this confession. 'I didn't mean to hurt you. It was so difficult, knowing that I was becoming more and more attracted to you, but feeling guilty that I had somehow contributed towards Juliette taking her own life. Then, when I realised that it wasn't suicide, I was only trying to protect you until I knew more about what was going on. So what made you realise I wasn't the culprit?'

'When the accidents started. You would never risk hurting Kirsty.'

He frowned. 'I suppose I should be grateful that I'm off your list.' He looked at her, one eyebrow raised. Then she realised that he was teasing her. She smiled wanly.

'Lewis, you've no idea what a strain this has been.'

He took her hand in his, squeezing it. 'We're in this together now. Let's see what we can work out.'

'There's something else — Mum thinks that Tim may be Michaela's son.' She told him what her mother had said about Michaela's past.

Lewis whistled. 'It hardly seems credible. But I suppose it could be. Do you think that has any bearing on these goings on?'

'I don't know. But Mum wonders why they've been keeping it a secret.'

'Well, basically it's none of our business. Why shouldn't they keep it to themselves?'

'I suppose you're right. Maybe we're looking for suspicious circumstances in every event.'

He put one arm round her. 'Well, don't worry about it now. We've got an emotional time for the next few days. I think we should try and put it to the back of our minds for a while.'

16

The next day, finding that she was alone in the house, Sonia decided to go up to her grandmother's room, to see if being there would bring her close for one last time.

Pushing the door, Sonia stepped into the room, and gasped at the sight that met her eyes. The bureau top was down, and there were papers scattered everywhere. One of the drawers lay on the floor, its contents strewn on the carpet.

Sonia knelt down to retrieve it, tears streaming down her face. It stung her to think that anyone could do such a thing to her grandmother's belongings. It didn't matter that she wasn't here any more. Wiping her cheeks, she worked at setting matters to rights. Gradually she sorted the papers, tucking them into their boxes and cubbyholes, then raised the lid and locked it with the tiny key.

There was some evidence that the rest of the room had been searched, but although it was rather untidy, it certainly hadn't been treated as badly as the bureau. It was as if the intruder had been angry at not finding what they had been seeking. Sonia tidied up generally, and didn't leave the room until she was satisfied that it was as neat as Felicity would have liked. If only they could find out the troubled secrets that were causing such destruction and ill-feeling, then her grandmother could be truly laid to rest.

She said nothing to Michaela when they began talking through arrangements for the funeral. However, she spoke to Lewis when he came home from work.

'I wonder if this is what they were looking for?' He handed a brown envelope to Sonia, addressed to her. 'I found it in my briefcase this morning. Felicity must have put it there after she spoke to you.'

Sonia slit it open to reveal a letter in a plain white envelope, and a note.

Dear Sonia, It read. I'm sending you this letter because I'm sure the wrong person overheard what I was saying to you. This explains such a lot. Perhaps you and Lewis can decide what to do now. I was wrong to suspect him. With love, Granny.

Sonia only had a moment to be thankful that her grandmother had decided to trust Lewis, before she turned her attention to the letter. It was an old one, postmarked London, but addressed to her grandfather, Michael Landale, and marked 'Personal'. Glancing at the signature, she saw that it was from Michaela. Then she began to read it.

Dear Uncle Michael,

I know you said not to write again, but I just had to. You've no idea how much I miss Alderburn. My 'little problem' is over now, and I've done what you wanted. So why can't I come home? I don't want to do a secretarial course. Not here, at least. Couldn't I do it at home?

Aunt Felicity won't let me come home either. She said you'd just put me straight back on a train to London, until I come back with a qualification. Nobody must know I've been a bad girl.

If you don't let me come back now, I'll tell everyone our little secret. No, not about my disgrace. Yes, I worked it out! That you're my real father, not your brother Bernard. After all, why else would my mother have named me after you?

Oh, please let me come home now! I can't bear to be away from Alderburn any longer.

With dearest love, from Michaela.

Sonia handed the letter to Lewis, who read it quickly. Looking up, he said, 'She doesn't say in as many words that she did have a baby — but that must be what she means by her 'little problem'.'

'Do you think the rest is true?'

'That Michael was her father? I thought you said that Felicity had denied it when she telephoned you.'

'Yes, she did. I believe her. It was probably just wishful thinking on the part of a girl who wanted to belong to Alderburn.'

'Michael must have persuaded her somehow not to carry out her threat to tell everyone. Maybe he did let her come home sooner. But it explains a lot,' he added. 'She's obviously more obsessed with the hall than I thought. I suppose she saw it going further and further away from her as it went first to Paul, then to Juliette.'

'And then to me and Kirsty.' She sat up and gazed at him in anguish. 'Oh, Lewis — surely Michaela can't be a murderer. Do you really believe she could have done away with Juliette for the sake of the house?'

Lewis sighed. 'I've lived in the same house as her for seven years, and I could never call her an evil person. She and Juliette were good friends. What's more, Juliette was leaving home when she was killed. It's possible she would never have returned here.'

'Somehow we're going to have to discover what really happened that night. But how?'

'I'll try to think of something. Let's wait a few days until your grandmother's funeral is over. I think we're getting a bit overwrought.'

Sonia nodded gratefully. As she looked into his eyes, she felt a strong current pass between them. There was a lot more to be said, but neither had the will to broach it now, their grief weighing too heavily.

Felicity's funeral took place a few days later at the Alderburn church. Sonia felt emotionally exhausted by the end of the day. She had asked Nicola to take Kirsty to her home for a few hours to keep her away from the funeral. The child had had too much to do with death in the past year. It had been enough to say that they were taking Granny to church to say goodbye to her.

'Will Granny look after Mummy in heaven?' the little girl asked hopefully.

Sonia's eyes pricked with tears. At last Kirsty seemed to have fully accepted her mother's death. 'Of course. They'll both look after each other, and now you know you'll have two people smiling down on you together.'

Kirsty nodded in a matter-of-fact way, then skipped off to find her bicycle. It was a relief to see her behave with the carelessness of childhood.

It was just after seven o'clock when the telephone rang. Lewis was in Alderburn collecting Kirsty, and Michaela had gone to her room early as she had a head-ache. Sonia decided to answer it.

'Is that . . . Alderburn Hall?' It was a man's voice.

'Yes.'

'Is it possible to speak to Juliette Gordon, please?'

Sonia gasped. 'Oh . . . well, didn't you know? Juliette died, last year.'

'What?' It was the turn of the caller

to sound shocked. 'I can't believe it — when? . . . I mean, how?'

'It was in May. She . . . drowned in the river.'

'How terrible! That explains why I never heard from her.' Then there was a pause. 'Who am I speaking to?'

'I'm her cousin, Sonia Landale.'

'Sonia! I didn't recognise your voice. It's Richard.'

'Richard?' For a moment she was mystified.

'Richard Hayling. Don't tell me you've forgotten me so soon.'

Richard! The man who had betrayed her with Juliette. Her voice took on a hard edge. 'I didn't realise you still kept in touch with her — you said it was a spur-of-the-moment thing.'

'It was — but later she asked me to act as a sort of post box for her. She stayed here once or twice when she was having singing lessons in London, and she had given this address to some people. Occasionally a letter would arrive, but she didn't want them sent on to her directly. I had to send her a text, then she would let me know where to send the letters. It was a different address each time. She didn't want me to ring the house. That's why I hesitated for so long.'

'You mean you have some letters?'

'Yes, there are three now. I sent a text when each arrived, but of course she never contacted me. That's why I decided to telephone. I was going to make up a story about being a musical friend. I don't know why she wanted so much secrecy.'

'Maybe it was just her sense of drama. Richard, what were the letters about?'

'I haven't opened them. Should I?'

Sonia hesitated. 'No. Would you send them to Lewis's office?' She gave him the address, then realised that she had no particular feelings at hearing Richard's voice — she felt quite free of the pain of his rejection. A surge of triumphant confidence ran through her. Only Lewis mattered to her now.

Sonia would have liked to speak to

Lewis as soon as he returned, but Kirsty was exhausted and clung to him tearfully. He smiled ruefully at Sonia, and carried the child up to bed as soon as she had drunk some warm milk.

Sonia tried to occupy herself for a while, flicking through the television channels, then decided to go upstairs to see if Kirsty was asleep yet. Lewis was leaving the nursery wing as she arrived.

'Sleeping?' she asked, raising her eyebrows.

'Absolutely sound. She was shattered. She was talking about Juliette again, saying she missed her. I think it's the loss of Felicity that's brought it all up again.'

'But she has grasped that she's gone, now.'

He sighed, pushing back his hair. 'Yes, she seems to. I feel she's so fragile emotionally. It must be so bewildering for her, losing two of her family within a year.'

'Poor Kirsty.' She remembered Richard's call, and decided it would be best to tell Lewis straight away. 'I've been speaking to Richard — you know, Richard Hayling. He telephoned this evening . . . '

'What's he doing sniffing round here again? I thought you said it was over with him!'

Sonia gasped, dismayed at his furious expression. 'You surely don't think . . . ? I just don't believe it! After what he did to me . . . He was speaking to me about Juliette.' She felt the tears rising, devastated that Lewis should think she still cared for Richard.

'They betrayed me, too.' They stood for a moment, fuming at each other. Then Lewis reached out, putting his hands on her shoulders. 'I can't believe we're talking like this. Oh, come here,' he added gently, pulling her into his arms.

Sonia responded by sliding her own arms around him. It was a comfort to feel the warmth of his body against hers. It had been so long since anyone had held her like this — and she knew that the only one she wanted to do so was Lewis.

His body trembled against hers. 'Let's not stand in the corridor — come in my room.' As soon as the door closed behind them, he took her in his arms again. Tilting her head back, he wiped the tears from her cheeks with one finger, then, touching her chin, he lowered his lips to hers. It was a tender kiss, which gradually became more heated, until they broke apart, gasping with mounting desire.

'Oh, Sonia, I'm sorry for being such a jealous fool. As if you really would go back to Richard. I just couldn't bear the thought of you belonging to anyone else.'

She pulled him close, resting her head on his shoulder. 'I only want to be with you. I think I loved you from the moment we first met, but it wasn't until recently that I realised that I couldn't live without you.'

'I feel that way, too. When I first met you, I realised that I had made a terrible mistake with Juliette. But we were committed, and she was expecting Kirsty. I often wonder if she suspected how I felt about you, and that was why she made a point of seducing Richard.'

Sonia looked up at him, surprised. 'Could that be possible? I thought it was just because she wanted to be part of the glamour of the theatrical world. I was the only person she knew in the profession, and Richard was the only male performer she had met.'

'Well, maybe that's so. But I do love you, and want you to marry me now, Sonia. Please say yes — it's not just for Kirsty, but I can't deny that she adores you, too.'

'No, I know it's because you want the hall. It'll be all done and dusted nicely, no legal complications.' She grinned mischievously.

He answered with a wry smile. 'We should be so lucky! That's something else I have to discuss with you. I received an offer this morning — a very fair offer. I think we should take it.' He took her hand and led her to sit beside him on the bed.

'For the hall?' Sonia's eyes were full of dismay. 'Oh, no, I'd tried to forget about it. And now we really do have to leave Alderburn Hall.'

He stroked her hair. 'I think I know a way out. I was going to suggest that you live in the cottage. There would be enough money from the sale of the hall to do it up nicely. But if it's going to be a family house, we'll have to include the derelict farm buildings as an extension. I'll apply for a mortgage. We can go down and look at it tomorrow. That is, of course, if you accept me? You haven't said yes, yet!'

'Oh, Lewis, of course the answer is yes! But the cottage — that sounds wonderful!'

They kissed tenderly, and once their initial fervour cooled, Lewis put his arm round her and drew her close. 'So, tell me, what was it that Richard told you about Juliette?'

Sonia explained the telephone call.

Lewis nodded. 'I hope he sends the

letters immediately. This could be vital information.'

They sat hugging each other for several minutes, then Sonia pushed away. 'I don't think we should be too open about the change in our relationship for a while.'

'I suppose you're right. But we'll tell your parents we're engaged, OK?'

'Yes.' She looked into his eyes, delighting in the warmth of love and longing that she read in their depths.

'Sonia . . . ' he murmured, touching her cheek tenderly. All at once they found they could hold back no longer. Consumed with desire, she returned his kisses passionately, and gasped with delight as he slid his hand under her top. He stroked her bare back, making her tingle with pleasure. She reached for his shirt, unbuttoning it and running her hands over his chest. Before they knew it, both were naked, exploring each other's bodies. Sonia responded to his touch with mounting pleasure, desperate for the fulfilment she had longed for. His tenderness became passion, his lean body taut with desire.

Lewis paused, poised to enter her, and whispered, 'Are you sure you want this, now?'

'Oh, yes, please, don't stop!'

Then he was inside her, their love fulfilled at last, their bodies as one. Afterwards, as the heat cooled and they lay entwined, he drew the cover over their nakedness. There was no need for words in the aftermath of their lovemaking.

After a while, Sonia stirred. 'I must go — otherwise I'll never be able to leave,' she said softly.

They couldn't resist another kiss, their bodies warm against each other. Finally Lewis groaned and sat up. 'Oh, this is so difficult! I wish we could forget the world and just be together.'

'As soon as this is sorted out, I promise we won't wait another day.'

Once she had dressed again, Sonia touched her glowing cheeks. 'I hope I don't meet anyone until I've cooled down a bit.'

A secret smile of intimacy passed between them. Lewis touched his lips to her hair, before opening the door a crack to survey the corridor. She slipped through the doorway, glancing back to his loving face for an instant before she hurried back towards her own room. Her whole body glowed with passion. How long would it be before they could be open about their love?

17

She told her parents quietly about their engagement. Teresa hugged her fiercely.

'I know this is right for you, dear. I'm so happy for you both.'

Dan added his own congratulations, and they agreed to keep it to themselves for the time being.

'After all, it's not so long since Juliette's death,' Sonia explained. 'We think we'll probably wait till the summer for the wedding. By then the sale of the house should be through, and the cottage will be ready.'

Lewis decided to hold back until the Saturday before telling Michaela about the house offer. He thought it would be too upsetting for her to hear it immediately after Felicity's funeral. Sonia was with him when he broke the news.

'This really is a very good offer for

the house and grounds. We really can't afford to turn it down.'

Michaela's eyes were hot with resentment. 'Is it a developer?'

'No, I'm pleased to say it's a private buyer. He's a businessman from the Midlands, head of a computing firm. I believe they're opening up a new place in the Gateshead area.'

The muscles of her mouth were tense. 'You were always determined to keep me out of this — both of you.' Her gaze flashed to Sonia, who felt a stab of guilt.

Michaela stood up. 'Well, now I know for sure that I'm going to lose my home, I need some time to think. I'm going away for a few nights. I'm sure you realise that's for the best, if we stay out of each other's way for a while.' She paused at the door and turned to them. 'I'd just like to know, Sonia, where you will be going. Are you returning to Canada with Teresa and Dan?'

Taken aback at the directness of her question, Sonia stammered, 'Well . . . no . . . Lewis thought we, I mean, I, might do up the cottage to live in . . . '

It was too late to hide her mistake. Michaela had already picked up on it. She gave them a long and searching look, before the corner of her mouth twitched. 'So that's what's going on. It doesn't surprise me — you never did have a second look for Tim.'

Without waiting for a reply, she opened the door and swept out of the room. Seeing Sonia biting her lip, Lewis pulled her close.

'Don't be upset. We knew it would be difficult.'

'But now she knows about us, when we had meant to keep it secret — and she'll tell Tim.'

He frowned. 'Does that bother you?'

'Not because I have any feelings for him. I never gave him any reason to hope, but I still think he hadn't given up on the idea that I might turn to him.'

Lewis sighed. 'He was bound to find out sooner or later. But I shouldn't worry. I expect Michaela will be with him for the next few days. We'll just try to stay out of their way as much as possible.'

The envelope containing Juliette's letters arrived two days later. They went into Lewis's office so that they could read them together. He examined the postmarks for dates, and chose the earliest one, dated July. It was an official-looking letter, with a foreign stamp. He read it quickly then passed it over to Sonia, his face inscrutable.

Dear Fräulein Landale

We see from our records that you did not take up your place on the Opernmeisterklass at the Opernakademie, Wien. As you know, your deposit is forfeit if no cancellation is received one month in advance.

Sonia gasped. 'Wien — Vienna. And I believe that means opera masterclass. Oh, Lewis, what an honour! I've heard that the really top names in opera teach on that course. It's for the best young singers of their generation.' Suddenly her eyes flooded with tears. 'What a waste, to think that she never got there!'

Instead she drowned in a swollen river, she thought sadly.

Lewis squeezed her hand. 'I know,' he stated simply, then reached for the next letter. It also had a foreign postmark. 'It's in German — I studied it at school, so I might be able to understand some of it.' He scrutinised it carefully. 'It's from the Vienna Opera. They're offering Juliette an audition, based on a CD she sent them. It's dated August.'

'I suppose it took them some time to get round to listening to an unsolicited application,' Sonia said. 'She would probably have been hoping to contact them once she reached Vienna.' She sighed, thinking of all the success that her cousin had missed. 'What's the third one, Lewis?'

'London postmark,' he told them. 'It's a Christmas card.' He opened it quickly. 'There's a message inside: *I sent the card to this address, as it's the only one I have for you. I've been longing to hear how you got on at the Vienna master-class. I'm so proud of you — none of my pupils has ever had that honour. Do keep in touch.* The card's signed *Alicia.*'

'It's not *that* common as a Christian name. Maybe we could find out something about her on the internet.'

Sonia went back to her desk and began searching for the name Alicia connected with singing in London. After a while she found an Alicia Turina registered as a singing teacher at one of the London music colleges. She also found her home number listed for singing coaching. Lewis had to go to court that morning, but promised to telephone Alicia when he returned. Sonia spent the rest of the morning on her work, but over lunchtime searched genealogy websites for birth records in London for the year of Tim's birth.

Sonia found an entry for a Michael Landale born six days before Michaela's letter was posted from London. She put in a request for a copy of the birth certificate, to be sent to Lewis's office. It was logical that Michaela should have named her son Michael, after the man who had obsessed her so much.

Sonia was finished for the day at three o'clock, and went to collect Kirsty from school. They played for a while with a ball on the lawn before coming in for Kirsty's tea. She was happily watching a favourite DVD when Lewis arrived home. After greeting his daughter, he motioned to Sonia to follow him.

'I managed to speak with Alicia Turina,' he said as he took her hand and pulled her into his study. He spoke in a low voice, and Sonia responded in a similar manner.

'So had she been Juliette's teacher?'

He nodded. 'She was devastated to hear of her death. What's more, she had never known that Juliette had a husband and child. I had to spend some time consoling her — she had taught Juliette for three years. Miss Turina thought she could have been a successful professional opera singer. Can you believe it? She kept it a secret all this time!'

Sonia shook her head, mystified. 'Why couldn't she tell anyone? She was always a drama queen.'

'But there's more that could be interesting. At Juliette's last lesson, a young man came to meet her at the door. Miss Turina saw him quite clearly, and, from the description, it sounds like Tim. Also, she said that he kissed her, quite passionately.'

Sonia gasped. 'So that could be the proof we need, that he was Juliette's lover. Was she quite clear?'

'Oh, yes. She described him with no prompting at all from me.'

'So what do we do now?' she asked.

'Well, I think we ought to look at the circumstantial evidence we've amassed so far.'

Sonia smiled to herself. He sounded so like a solicitor.

'Let's start with your findings in Durham,' he began. 'The main piece of evidence we have is the suitcase and clothes that were replaced in Juliette's room.'

' . . . And the opera score.'

'Yes, it must have been one she was

studying for the masterclass. Also, now we have proof that she wasn't planning on ending her own life — she was going to Vienna to study.'

'But where does Tim come into this? Even though we know that they were obviously involved, it doesn't look as if Juliette had included him in her plans.'

'Well, let's consider Michaela. She had believed for a long time that she was Michael Landale's daughter — which meant that once your father and uncle died, she believed she was his last surviving child. Juliette inherited the hall, but Michaela obviously thought that she had more of a right to it. And once she was reunited with her son, she had a reason to want it even more.'

'But I can't believe that she could kill anyone, even if she did long for the hall. Anyway, she was in London the night of Juliette's death, and I've no doubt it could be proved from a hotel register.'

'That's true. But we don't know Tim's whereabouts. Was he supposed to help Juliette with her arrangements?

Was there an accident somehow? But if it was an accident, why didn't they just leave the suitcase at the station for us to discover at a later date? Or was there some incriminating evidence in it?'

'Maybe it just suited them to have the verdict of suicide.'

'It certainly made things much tidier. They would need to return the clothes so that no-one would realise that she had packed a case. I expect that your arrival prompted them to do that — not realising that you had already searched the room for the opera score.'

'But there's something else — what about the 'accidents' that targeted Kirsty and me?'

Lewis's face was grim. 'You're right. That's when things became more sinister. Kirsty *is* in danger, and you, too. Let's not leave her alone any longer.' He went to open the study door, and they began to climb the stairs to the nursery wing. 'Those incidents happened once the sale of the hall became more imminent. I wonder if it would have made any difference if we had let Michaela in as a co-owner?' Kirsty ran to Lewis as they entered the nursery, and he sat down, taking her on his knee.

Sonia sat next to them, picking up Kirsty's plush rabbit and fondling its ears absently. 'But you said yourself that it wouldn't work.'

'I know.' He sighed, pushing the child's coppery hair back from her forehead. 'Also, it might have put her in a better position to inherit, had anything happened to you two.'

Kirsty realised that they were talking about adult things, which bored her, so she reached for Mr. Rabbit before going back to sit on the floor in front of the television set. She reached to stroke her cat, curled up asleep on a cushion beside her. Soon she was engrossed in the film again, chewing the rabbit's ear absently.

Sonia continued in an undertone, too quiet for Kirsty to hear above the sound of the television. 'So what can we do? We haven't any real proof at all. We think that Tim is most likely to be involved somehow in Juliette's — accident — but we only suspect that Michaela is connected. It's not a crime to have had an illegitimate child. It's only my word that the suitcase and clothes reappeared in the bedroom. If we produce the letters from Vienna it'll only change the verdict to accidental death.'

'I know. There's really nothing we can do, except to try and push through the sale as quickly as possible. Then the problem will be out of our hands. Once the hall is sold, she couldn't inherit it, only buy it back.'

'Or we could confront them — but it sounds so far-fetched, and almost malicious on our part. I just wish the whole thing would go away. I don't want to think that someone I know could kill anyone else, or wish to harm Kirsty and me.'

Lewis took her hand and pressed it. 'The main thing is that we've got all the evidence we can find, and I'll put it away safely in the office, in case we need it.'

She squeezed his fingers. 'Yes, that would be best.'

He pulled her towards him and kissed her tenderly on the lips. 'Well, we'd better put on a brave face for now.' The DVD was finishing. Kirsty stood up and ran towards them, throwing herself into their arms. They smiled and laughed with her, pushing aside any serious thoughts for a while.

The birth certificate arrived within a few days, and confirmed that Michaela Landale was the mother of the baby named Timothy Landale, and that his father was a student. The father's name meant nothing to them, and was in fact irrelevant to their investigations.

There was plenty to do to get the cottage ready in time to move in. They had set a time span of two months, and a friend of Lewis's who specialised in conversions and conservation work was drafted in to plan and supervise the building. By the time it was finished they would have a lovely home with three large bedrooms and an attic room, which Kirsty was already calling her own.

Lewis kept Michaela informed of the progress of the sale. The atmosphere was strained, so they stayed apart as much as possible. Lewis and Sonia kept their relationship to themselves, not openly showing any affection in company. Sonia's office job finished as the original typist returned to work. Apart from the coaching at the ballet school, she was spending much of her time at the Northumbrian Ballet, working as advisor on Richard's ballet. It was revitalising, and she had less time to think about the trials of the house sale.

Her mother and stepfather returned to Canada a few weeks after New Year. Tim hadn't appeared in January, as he was attending a major football event in Manchester. Sonia was relieved that he was out of the way. Now that he had proved to be the one most likely to be involved in Juliette's death, he had become frightening to her.

Lewis had an important case on in Leeds the following week. The Northumbrian Ballet had a major dress rehearsal which coincided with Lewis's last day in court, so Nicola's mother had kindly offered to collect Kirsty and take her home for a while. Nicola was at college full-time now, but she and her mother would bring the little girl home and would put her to bed if Lewis hadn't arrived in time. Nicola would stay as long as she was needed, and one of them would take her home later.

Feeling exhausted but exhilarated, Sonia turned into the drive at about quarter to nine in the evening. There had been some technical hitches with the costumes and the rehearsal had gone on longer than intended, but it had finally been sorted out. The first night would be on Tuesday, and there was a buzz about the company that this would be a great success.

She put the car into the barn, then walked over to the hall. As she entered the front door, Michaela appeared from the drawing room.

'Oh, Sonia, Lewis got back about half an hour ago. He's gone down to the cottage and asked me to tell you to meet him there as soon as you can.'

Sonia frowned. 'What on earth could he want with me down at the cottage at this time of night? It'll be freezing.'

Michaela shrugged. 'Well, of course, he didn't tell me. But he said there was something he needed to look at. Maybe you have to make some decisions before the workmen come in tomorrow.'

'I suppose it must be. Well, I'd better change my shoes. I'll just walk down. He didn't take the flashlight, did he?'

'No, I think he took the car.'

'Of course — it wasn't in the barn.'

There was a strong wind, making the branches sigh and heave around her, but at least it was dry. *Why on earth couldn't he wait until I got home?* she thought grumpily. Her fatigue was beginning to catch up with her. It would have been so nice just to curl up with a hot drink in front of the fire.

Finally she could see a light through the trees. As she neared the cottage, she realised that the lit window was the main upstairs bedroom, the one that she and Lewis had chosen for their own. The front door was ajar.

'Lewis?' she called as she pushed it open. She could hear movement above her, and began to climb the stairs. 'Is that you, Lewis?'

She walked into the bedroom, where a solitary light burned. At first the room seemed to be empty, then she heard the door close behind her. Swinging round, she cried out when she saw who was in the room with her. 'Michaela! What's going on? Where's Lewis?'

Michaela laughed, but it had an unpleasant edge. 'You fell right into the trap! You always were a little innocent!'

'Trap? I don't understand . . . '

'Lewis isn't here at all. He rang me this afternoon because he said that your phone wasn't switched on, and he wanted to make sure that you would get his message, as he says you're always forgetting to switch it back on after rehearsals. The hearing is going on later than they thought, which means that he won't be back before eleven. It was then that I realised this was a golden opportunity.' She looked very satisfied with herself.

'To . . . to do what?' Sonia was beginning to feel increasingly apprehensive. She eyed the door, wondering if she could somehow barge past Michaela, but the older woman was standing with her hand on the door handle, and there was no way she could get by her.

'To remove the final barriers to Tim's inheritance. Oh, yes, I know you've been prying into my past. Well, I'm not afraid to recognise him as my son now. He persuaded me to keep quiet about it for a while to see if we could get a stake in the hall. I wish I'd never let them persuade me to give him up when he was a baby. It seemed a good idea at the time — Tony, his father, wasn't interested in settling down with kids. I just wanted to get the business over with, and back to Alderburn.' Her face suddenly changed, becoming perplexed. 'But then when Juliette and you were born, I began to think of my little boy, and began to wonder what he looked like, and if he knew about me. And when Aidan and Paul died, I realised then that I'd given away the heir to Alderburn. *Girls!*' she exclaimed in disgust. 'No good for the hall. No skinny little girl is going to do my son out of his inheritance.'

Sonia felt a surge of anger. 'So you *were* behind Juliette's death, and the other 'accidents'.'

Michaela shrugged. 'The accidents, yes. But not Juliette. That wasn't intended.' Her eyes grew hard. 'The little slut led Tim on. She told him that she'd run away with him, and when Lewis had given her a divorce, she'd marry him. But she was just using him to make all her arrangements, so no one in the hall would know what she was up to. He even took her suitcase to the station. The arrangement was to meet her at the bridge. Then she told him she didn't care about him, it was just the singing. Naturally, he got angry. He didn't mean to push her so hard . . . '

'And he just left her, to drown?' Sonia's voice was shocked.

'She was dead before she reached the water — her head hit a rock. He pushed her further down the river so that she wouldn't be found immediately. It was easy to make it look like an accident.' Her lips curved. 'But it was fortuitous that she had left such an ambiguous note. It really made it look as if she wanted to do away with herself. But when you arrived, I realised that Lewis would ask you to go through her clothes, so we had to collect the case and put her things back in her room.'

' . . . But I'd already looked in, and noticed when they were replaced. That's what made me believe what Granny told me — that Juliette would never take her own life. It was she who put the idea into my head that someone else had caused her death.'

Michaela's features dropped in incredulity. 'Felicity? But she was so frail . . .'

'There was nothing wrong with Granny's mind, as you know full well,' Sonia stated harshly. 'But I can only be glad that she never found out the truth.'

'No-one's going to find out the truth. There's going to be a convenient accident, in an unoccupied house where building work is going on. Quite plausible.'

'Lewis won't believe it.'

'Well, he won't be able to prove anything.' Then she looked round, listening. Footsteps sounded on the stairs. 'Ah, here we are.'

She pulled the door open, to admit Tim. Sonia gasped when she saw that he was carrying the sleeping Kirsty. 'No, not Kirsty! Do what you like to me, but she's only a child.'

Michaela turned back to her savagely. 'But she owns half the house. If Tim is to get it — through me — then she has to die as well.'

'Tim . . . please!' Sonia begged.

He laid the sleeping child on the floor. 'If you'd been more compliant, we could have spared you. If you'd married me, then I would have got the house anyway. Michaela deserves it, not you. She looked after Felicity for years, and was a real daughter to Michael. You did nothing except sponge.'

'That's not true! And I never asked to inherit the house. It was as much a surprise to me as it was to you.'

'That's plain, now that you're selling it to strangers,' Michaela stated bitterly. 'Enough chatter. Fix the lights, Tim.'

Michaela fetched a large oil-lamp from the corner, and lit it. Sonia recognised it as being the lamp from Felicity's room. Trying to rouse Kirsty, she shook her, more and more strongly.

'There's no point even trying — she won't wake. I gave her part of a sleeping pill in her bedtime milk. She didn't taste it because I put plenty of sugar in.'

'And how did you get her away from Nicola?'

'I told her that Lewis had just phoned to say that he was almost at Durham, and that Tim was to take her home, so that she wasn't kept too late. She was a bit reluctant until I told her she could ride on the motorbike.' Her mouth twisted contemptuously. 'Shallow fool!'

At that moment they were plunged into darkness, save for the glow of the oil lamp.

'Ah, well done, Tim.'

Sonia gathered Kirsty into her arms. Tim reappeared with a torch, nodding grimly at Michaela. 'Come on, we'd better get on with it.'

Without another word, Michaela dropped the oil lamp. A patch of flaming oil spread across the floor towards Sonia. Panicking, she turned to the window and began hauling at the boards that covered it. Suddenly she felt a blow to the side of her head, and was vaguely aware as she sank to the floor, that Tim had punched her.

18

Sonia came round gasping for breath in the blazing room. Her head throbbed. Dragging herself to her knees, she crawled over to the unconscious Kirsty, to pull her as far as she could from the flames.

There seemed to be a wall of fire between them and the door. Searching frantically for a way through, in the end she turned back to the window. It had been boarded up as the men were to put new glass in soon. She now knelt up, stretching as far as she could to try and haul away some of the wood. Her breath burned in her lungs with the effort. She managed to get hold of the end of one plank, and pulled it. The wood splintered halfway across, and with another effort, she managed to detach the whole plank.

But when she reached higher for the next plank, she found herself gasping for breath, and fell back to the floor, her lungs heaving. A flame caught at her skirt, and she beat it back, terrified. Sobbing with despair, she gathered Kirsty to her, trying to think how they could get out.

At that moment, the door burst open, bringing fresh oxygen to the flames, which surged higher. Sonia screamed, then as she made out the shape of Lewis, shrieked his name above the roar of the fire. He threw a rug over the flames, which gave him a path to them, then dragged Kirsty from her arms.

'Follow me!' he yelled.

Heat surging at them on both sides, they ran through the fire to the stairs, and out of the cottage into the blessed fresh air. As the cold air hit Sonia, she staggered, but Lewis wouldn't let her falter, grasping her arm until he had them at a safe distance from the cottage. In the distance the sound of sirens could be heard approaching.

'Are you hurt? What about Kirsty?' He looked anxiously into the face of his unconscious daughter.

'Michaela drugged her with a sleeping tablet.' Her voice was hoarse with the smoke.

Lewis raised one of Kirsty's eyelids. 'Her pupils don't look too dilated — but I'm not qualified to know. I'd better phone for an ambulance. What about you?'

'I . . . I think I'm OK. Tim hit me — I don't know how long I was out. My chest's a bit sore, too.'

'That's the smoke,' he said grimly as he strode over to the car to get his mobile. At that moment, two fire engines swept into the lane with an ear-splitting wail of sirens. Sonia hugged the child to her while Lewis phoned for an ambulance, then spoke to the chief fire officer.

'Her pulse seems steady,' she told him when he returned to them.

'What the hell happened in there?' he demanded. 'How did you get to be in the cottage with Kirsty at this time of night? I discovered that she was missing when I went into her room — then I saw the fire from the nursery window, and got over here as fast as I could.'

Quickly, she explained what had happened. By the time she had finished, Lewis's face was creased in a deep frown. 'It looks as if the police should have been involved, too. I'd better go up to the house immediately. The fire officers will stay with you until the ambulance arrives — it won't be long.'

'Lewis . . . ' She reached out for him as he turned to go. 'Take care — if Michaela and Tim know you found us in time, they could harm you, too.'

He kissed her gently. 'I'll be wary, don't worry.'

Tears pricked her eyes as she watched him drive away. 'Hurry back, Lewis,' she whispered as she cradled his daughter in her arms.

Lewis caught up with her in Casualty at the hospital, where she was sitting in a cubicle beside Kirsty, who was sleeping. 'What did they say? How's Kirsty?'

'They say she'll be fine — she'll just sleep heavily and wake feeling a bit woozy. They want us both to stay overnight to monitor us for the effects of smoke inhalation.' Seeing his face relax, she continued, 'What happened at the hall?'

He shook his head. 'Nothing — they've gone. They must have been packed and ready to leave as an alibi before the so-called 'accident' occurred. I expect they'll go into hiding somewhere, possibly abroad.'

Sonia laid her head on his shoulder, tears now overflowing from her eyes. 'How could this have happened, Lewis? How could someone so close to me turn on us all?' The sentence ended with a bout of coughing, her voice hoarse and irritated from the smoke.

He circled her with his arms. 'Hush, love. You have to accept that Michaela was very emotionally damaged, by the tragedies in her life. She was obsessed with the hall, and obsessions can make people do cruel things. Remember, she thought she was protecting her son's interests — the threatened tigress.'

'Will the police find them? I don't quite know how I feel about them going to prison.'

'I'll play it down as much as possible, if that's what you want.'

She nodded, wiping her eyes. 'As long as we're left alone, and we're safe, that's all I want. I don't want all this to be dragged through the newspapers. Just imagine how it could affect Kirsty at school, and in later life when she's old enough to understand.'

'I know. It's time to put the past behind us, now. The cottage isn't badly damaged, and as soon as it's ready, we'll move in. Our future is all prepared.'

★ ★ ★

The late August sunshine flooded the kitchen as Sonia set the knives and forks at the table ready for their evening meal. Lewis was upstairs changing out of his suit. Mitten, Kirsty's tabby cat, was eating daintily from a bowl by the back door. It was through this that her owner erupted, calling out.

'Mummy, there's a policeman asking for you at the front. He's got a lovely car, and there's a police lady with him, too.'

It always gave Sonia a thrill to hear Kirsty call her 'Mummy'. She had started of her own accord as soon as they had been married, saying that now Sonia was her daddy's wife, she had to be her mummy. When Sonia pointed out that she had had a real mother, she said that Juliette was her mummy in heaven, and Sonia her mummy on Earth. It had brought a lump to Sonia's throat.

Sonia went to the front door to meet the police officers, her heart pounding. At least she knew that nothing had happened to Lewis — she would have been terrified if he hadn't been safely home.

'Mrs. Sonia Gordon? Formerly Miss Landale?'

'Yes?'

'May we come in? We have some news for you concerning your relation

Miss Michaela Landale, and her son, Timothy Warren-Landale.

With a gasp, Sonia ushered them in. 'Of course, please go into the living room. It's through here. Kirsty, would you please get Daddy from upstairs? Tell him it's very important.'

Lewis was down within moments.

'Mrs. Gordon, you have been traced as being the nearest living relation of Miss Michaela Landale.'

'Has something happened to her?' Sonia broke in.

'Yes, we're sorry to have to bring you bad news. She and her son were involved in a road accident in the south of France and didn't survive. The French police traced Miss Landale's address to Alderburn Hall, and when we called there, the new owners directed us here.'

Sonia slipped her hand into Lewis's. 'Have Tim's adoptive parents been told?'

'Yes, they were also traced.'

Lewis held her hand tightly. 'Thank you, officer. We had wondered what happened to Michaela and Tim when they left suddenly. There'd been . . . some estrangement.'

With a few more formalities, the police officers left. Lewis and Sonia sat quietly for a moment.

'Oh, Lewis, what a sad end to their lives. Tim had such talent, too. I'm sorry things went the way they did.'

'I know, love. It's been a tragic time in the history of the Landales. I think it was inevitable that they would go that way. They both loved fast living, and I don't think either of them would have enjoyed growing old.'

'I know. I think you're probably right.'

There was silence for a few moments, as they sat, engrossed in their own thoughts. Then Lewis asked, 'What are you thinking? Your face looks so clouded.'

'Just what you said about it being a sad chapter in the history of our family. I sometimes feel that I took over everything that was Juliette's — her house, her husband, and her child. It's almost as if I was dancing on her grave, you know?'

Indignant, he sat up. 'You mustn't think that. After all, Juliette was leaving all of it behind to pursue her own interests. And remember what Felicity told you — Juliette was sorry for causing your accident, and realised that she had behaved selfishly. She must have felt that in leaving the house to you, she was making it up to you in some way. Of course, she would never have expected you to inherit so soon. But I'm sure, if she knew, she would be satisfied with the way things have turned out.'

'Do you really think so?'

'I certainly do.' He stroked her hair. 'I've been thinking, you know. How would you feel about opening a new chapter in the history of the Gordon family?'

She turned to him, her face beginning to light with understanding. 'Are you saying what I think you are?'

'Don't you think it would be nice for our family to start growing?' His eyes were warm.

She hesitated, keeping him in suspense. 'Well, you know, I have my career . . . '

His smile faltered.

' . . . But I expect I could put it on hold for a while.' She reached for him, pulling him close. She smiled contentedly over his shoulder, watching through the window the child playing in the garden and hoping that soon there would be two . . .

THE END